Kira Snapped The Breech Of The Gun Closed.

Jason Bearclaw stopped dead in his tracks. "The Navaho are a peaceful people, Mrs. Lowell," he said. "We don't take scalps. I've come to see my son."

"You gave him life, but my husband and I raised him as our own."

"A man has a right to see his child. It's the way of nature." He started toward her, so Kira pointed the weapon directly at his midsection. "Do you plan to shoot me?" he asked.

"I'm letting you know you can't come on my ranch and disregard my wishes."

"I'm concerned about my son. I worry that he's being raised in ignorance of his heritage. I want to know him. Is that unreasonable?"

"Let's be honest," she snapped, waving the muzzle of the gun. "Your intention isn't to get to know Toby. You want to take him from me."

Dear Reader:

I hope you've been enjoying 1989, our "Year of the Man" at Silhouette Desire. Every one of the twelve authors who are contributing a *Man of the Month* has created a very special someone for your reading pleasure. Each man is unique, and each author's style and characterization give you a different insight into her man's story.

From January to December, 1989 will be a twelve-month extravaganza spotlighting one book each month with special cover treatment as a tribute to the Silhouette Desire hero—our *Man of the Month*!

Created by your favorite authors, these men are utterly captivating—and I think Mr. June, Annette Broadrick's Quinn McNamara, will be simply...*Irresistible*! One of Lass Small's Lambert sisters gets a very special man in July. *Man of the Month* Graham Rawlins may start as the *Odd Man Out*, but that doesn't last long....

Yours,

Isabel Swift

Senior Editor & Editorial Coordinator

JANICE KAISER
Moon Shadow

Silhouette Desire
Published by Silhouette Books New York
America's Publisher of Contemporary Romance

SILHOUETTE BOOKS
300 East 42nd St., New York, N.Y. 10017

ISBN: 0-373-05503-X

First Silhouette Books printing June 1989

Printed in the U.S.A.

Books by Janice Kaiser

Silhouette Special Edition

Borrowed Time #466
The Lieutenant's Woman #489

Silhouette Desire

The Rookie Princess #483
Moon Shadow #503

JANICE KAISER

Four years ago Janice Kaiser combined two new beginnings in her life: her second marriage and the start of her writing career. A former attorney, Ms. Kaiser is frequently asked if she misses law. "The answer is no," says the author of over ten books. "I prefer the creativity and freedom of writing." An experienced traveler, Ms. Kaiser likes to set her novels in places she's been to and loved. She always tries to ground her romances with realistic touches and says her first concern is the reader's pleasure.

For my C.D. from his D.D.,
with all my love

One

Kira Lowell looked up the long stretch of road running down the broad valley. On either side of the highway were hay fields, most of them mowed, many with bales scattered around that looked like children's blocks on a large table. In other places cattle grazed lazily in the late afternoon sun.

Toby hadn't said anything for several minutes. Kira glanced over at the boy, wondering what he was thinking. He stared straight ahead, his black hair shining in the sunlight coming through the side window. The only sounds were the Jeep's engine and the hum of the tires on the pavement.

Kira hated seeing them upset, but she hadn't seen any way to avoid telling him his natural father was headed for Oregon and could show up any day, any hour. Better the child was forewarned than surprised by the arrival of a man he'd never seen.

And it wasn't as though Kira herself was indifferent to the prospect. She feared it more than Toby, but for very different reasons. The man represented a threat to her role as the boy's adoptive mother, though exactly how, she couldn't say. But she'd sensed it in the tone of his letters.

The latest had been delivered that morning. He had minced no words. "I'm coming to see my son." There was no more asking permission, no more diplomatic requests. He was as definite as he could be.

The announcement had sent her into a panic. Alone on the ranch, she had visions of having to run the man off with threats, and even force, if necessary. Whatever it took, she was determined to stop him any way she could.

That afternoon, after she'd gotten control of herself, she decided to drive into Seneca Falls to see Conrad Willoughby, the lawyer who'd handled the settlement of her parents' estate the year before. Willoughby wasn't in his office, but she had tracked him down at Cattlemen's Restaurant, where the Lions Club met every Monday. The meeting was just breaking up when Kira spotted him at the cash register.

"You want what?" the lawyer had said in response to her request. He was a paunchy man of about sixty, with thin dark hair combed straight back. He had known her father for longer than her twenty-nine years.

"A court order to keep a man away from the ranch," she repeated.

A deep frown crossed the lawyer's face. "Who? What man?"

Kira sighed, feeling her shoulders slump. "Toby's father."

Willoughby's eyebrows rose. "You mean, his Indian father?"

"Yes, his natural father." Saying the words almost made her feel like crying.

"What's he done?"

"Nothing, yet. But he managed to track us down and wrote to me, asking to see Toby. I answered that at some point it might be all right, but I didn't think now was the best time. Toby's been through quite a bit, and it would be a lot to handle. He's only eight."

"This fellow took exception to your wishes, I gather."

She nodded, then told him about the letter that had arrived that morning. "He hasn't exactly threatened to do anything bad, but there's a certain menace in his tone. Is there some way I can keep him away from us...off the ranch?"

The lawyer pondered her words, turning the cigar he'd just bought round and round in his fingers. "You feel he's dangerous?"

"I don't know," Kira said. "I've never met the man."

Willoughby's eyebrows rose again.

"When Dan and I adopted Toby, his mother said she didn't know who the father was. We found out later that she was lying. He had left the reservation, and nobody knew where he was. By then the adoption proceedings were already completed, so Dan and I figured it didn't matter.

"Now, out of the blue, he's written. He claims he didn't know his girlfriend was pregnant and didn't find out about Toby until recently, after he returned to the reservation. He said he decided to track us down so that he could see his son."

Conrad Willoughby rubbed his chin thoughtfully. "What's this fellow's name?"

"Joshua Bearclaw. From what I'm able to gather, he's a lawyer now, just passed the bar. Apparently, he left to get an education and ended up in law school."

"A lawyer, eh? And you feel he's a danger to the boy?"

"Toby knows he's adopted, of course. He's aware there are people out there responsible for his existence, apart from Dan and me. But I don't know if he's ready to contend with a father he never expected to see. My preference would be for it to happen when Toby's eighteen and can decide for himself whether he wants to meet this man."

"And Bearclaw didn't buy it."

"That's right. The letter says he's on his way."

"Well, I probably can get a restraining order on him, if the boy's welfare is at stake. But that would mean serving him, and we can't do that until he shows up...if he does."

"So there's nothing I can do if he turns up on my doorstep?"

"If he gets out of line, you call the sheriff. Short of that, I can have some papers ready. But like I say, we have to find him here in Oregon first."

Kira looked bewildered.

"These situations can be nasty, I know," Willoughby said. "But in my experience, it's best if the people involved sit down and talk reasonably. Unless Bearclaw is some kind of nut, you might be just as well-off to try and deal with him, work out a compromise. I don't know how convinced you are that Toby's meeting his father would be bad. But if you can see a way to do it, and he'll go away satisfied, it might be the best solution."

"I've thought about that, Mr. Willoughby. The problem is his attitude. His letters are full of talk about Indian culture, Indian rights, exploitation by the white man—that sort of thing. I'm afraid he'll be disruptive."

"Hmm. You're saying this Bearclaw fellow is an activist."

"At the very least, he's a passionate man. Maybe that's what worries me."

And Bearclaw's passion *had* worried her. Ever since her conversation that afternoon with Conrad Willoughby, she'd mulled over her alternatives. None of them appealed to her. She rolled down the window of the Jeep a bit more to let some cooling air in and glanced again at her son.

"Will my father look like me?" Toby asked.

"I don't know, honey. I've never seen him."

He reflected. "Not even before I was born?"

"No. Daddy and I didn't even know your birth mother until you were almost a year old."

"I wish they were both dead, instead of Daddy."

"It's nice to still love your father, but we don't ever want to wish anyone dead. You're feeling a little confused, is all. I understand that. It's natural."

"Couldn't you just tell him to go away?"

"I tried, but he wants very much to see you. If he does come, I'll explain the way we feel, and maybe he'll leave. But I decided it was best to tell you about him. I didn't think it was right to keep it a secret."

Toby smiled for the first time that afternoon, and Kira reached over and patted him on the cheek, letting her fingers linger affectionately.

"You're a smart boy," she said. "And very brave. I'm sure we'll be able to handle whatever happens."

He nodded, then looked out the window vacantly. "Mom," he said after a while, "what's my Indian father's name?"

"Joshua."

"Is that a Navaho name?"

"No, not necessarily. Not all Indians have Indian-sounding names, honey."

"Is it his first or his last name?"

"His first. His family name is Bearclaw."

"That's funny." He put his finger to his cheek thoughtfully. "If I was still an Ind . . . I mean, if this Indian father I have...didn't run away when I was born, would my name be Bearclaw, too?"

"Yes, I suppose it would." Kira could see the confusion already setting in. It hurt to think her son might be subjected to more. She caressed his cheek again.

"I'm glad he ran away, then," he said. "If my name was Toby Bearclaw, everybody at school would really laugh."

"The children don't make fun of you, do they?"

"No, not anymore. Maybe a little when I was new, but not much. Kids make fun of everybody when they're new."

"I suppose that's true. It's not very fair, but it does happen, I know." Kira hesitated, not knowing whether it was better to drop the subject or try to help Toby understand as much as possible. "But there is something new I've learned about your father—your birth father. He didn't run away like your dad and I thought. He didn't know you were going to be born before he left. Your mother didn't tell him."

The boy screwed up his face with confusion. "How come he didn't know? Doesn't he know how babies are born and all that stuff?"

Kira couldn't help laughing. "Yes, honey, he knows. Sometimes ladies don't tell the father there's a baby inside. And sometimes they don't know themselves for a long time."

"You mean, it's a surprise?"

"Yes," she said, tousling his hair. "Sometimes it's a very big surprise."

"I'm not going to have any surprises when I grow up," Toby said. "And I'm not going to get married. I'm going to be a navy fighter pilot, just like Daddy."

"Daddy would be very proud of you," Kira said, fighting back a bubble of emotion.

Toby saw that her eyes had filled with tears. He reached over and patted her arm. "That was the saddest day in our whole life, when Daddy's plane crashed, wasn't it, Mom?"

Kira sniffled, holding back the tears. "Yes, honey, it certainly was."

The sun was setting behind the mountains when they turned off the highway under the arched wood sign identifying the Adamson Ranch. Kira saw no point in changing it. The property would bear her parents' name until it was sold.

As they drove past, she glanced at the large double-sided For Sale sign near the entrance. One of the braces had broken, causing it to list. She made a mental note to call the real estate broker and have it fixed. It was bad enough that the property had been on the market for almost a year; there was no point in giving the ranch a dilapidated appearance when it was undeserved.

Sam Adamson had been a top-notch rancher and made sure everything was kept in good repair. If it hadn't been for the depression in agriculture, the place would have sold long ago. But times being what they were, many ranchers considered themselves lucky not to lose their land to the banks.

Kira had had an offer the previous spring, but it was at a sacrifice price. Fortunately the loan her father had on the property was an old one, and she was able to keep up the payments simply by leasing out the land.

As they went along the bumpy driveway leading to the ranch house, the sacks of groceries in the back of the Jeep began rattling.

"With this old driveway, it's a wonder we don't have half our eggs broken," she said to her son.

Toby grinned. "Then you wouldn't have to scramble them."

Kira smiled in response as she looked at her watch. "I thought I was doing you a favor, picking you up at school, but you're getting home much later than if you'd taken the bus."

"That's because we were in the dumb old supermarket forever."

"I had my big shopping to do. You know that always takes longer."

"It's dumb."

"Well, it's not so dumb when you're hungry."

"What's for dinner?"

Kira laughed. "I thought my logic might appeal to you."

"Can we have hamburgers?"

"I'm afraid not. Rod's coming for dinner. We'll have something special."

Toby stuck out his lower lip in an obvious pout. She knew that it wasn't so much the hamburgers as the mention of Rod Banyon that disappointed her son.

She had been dating Rod the past few months, and when she had run into him on her way to Cattlemen's, she had invited him to dinner. Kira had been promising him a home-cooked meal for quite a while. Besides, after Joshua Bearclaw's letter, the thought of having a man around, if only for the evening, was reassuring.

Still, deep down, she shared some of her son's uneasiness about Rod. He was one of the more prominent young men in Seneca Falls, owning two local car dealerships plus a number of commercial buildings. And he was good-looking, with a head of brownish-blond hair, an athletic frame and a rugged square jaw. Rod had been a bachelor for nearly two years, having divorced his wife before Kira returned to the area. He had a big condominium on the golf course, though he always ate out, prompting her dinner invitation.

"Does he *have* to come?" Toby groaned.

"Don't you like Rod?"

"He tells stupid jokes."

"That's hardly a reason to dislike someone."

"It is if you don't like stupid jokes."

Kira shrugged. "That's hard to dispute."

The boy's feelings weren't too disappointing, though, because Kira had almost decided nothing serious would come of their relationship. Rod was considered quite a catch, but she had never developed a true romantic interest in him, though she had promised herself to keep an open mind. She wondered, though, if it wasn't hopeless. After Dan, she didn't see how there could be anyone else.

They had gone most of the mile between the highway and the ranch house and were nearing the bluff where their home sat overlooking the valley. Kira had grown up on the place and had always loved it, so it hadn't been a hardship to come back and look after the ranch until it sold. She didn't like giving up the house in San Diego she had shared with her husband, but it had been comparatively easy to sell, and she had rationalized that some time in the country would be good for both Toby and her.

The Jeep wound up the flank of the bluff. When they crested the rise, the house came into view. Then, suddenly, she came to a stop. Sitting out in front was a car—one she'd never seen before. It was an ordinary American-made sedan, but it appeared to be empty. Her first thought was of Joshua Bearclaw.

She sat staring, her mind churning.

"Whose car is that?" Toby asked.

"I don't know, honey." Kira looked around at the trees, the porch of the house, then toward the outbuildings in the draw to the south. She saw no one, no sign—except for the car—that anyone was there. The thought that Joshua Bearclaw might be on the ranch sent a tremor of fear through her. Kira looked at her son. "Toby, you stay in the Jeep. I'm going to find out who's here."

"I'll come, too," he said.

"No. Mommy wants you to wait right here. Please. I'll lock the door. You stay inside, and don't come out until I tell you to. Understand?"

He nodded. Kira stepped out onto the gravel surface of the driveway. She put the key in the lock and turned it, securing her son inside.

The air was still. Behind them, the sky was aglow with red, orange and violet hues. With the sun nearly gone, the temperature was beginning to drop. She started walking toward the car, her gaze darting among it and the house and the trees. It had to be Toby's father, she reasoned. Strangers didn't come to the ranch.

The plates on the car were for Oregon, but when she got closer she could see by the sticker on the bumper that it was a rental. That made sense. Bearclaw could have flown into Medford, rented a car and driven over Hayden Pass.

Before she continued on, Kira looked back to the Jeep. Toby's face was close to the windshield. Again she peered into the deepening shadows under the trees. She wasn't sure why she felt he was in the woods. Perhaps it was because of his culture, the mystery of the man, her own imaginings.

Kira continued on toward the car, her boots crunching on the gravel. Perhaps he was snoozing in the back seat. He may have been waiting for them half the day, and grown tired.

When she peered in the car, it was empty. The door on the driver's side was unlocked, so she opened it. The keys were in the ignition. A half-open map was on the passenger seat, and a worn overnight bag was in back. Kira closed the car door and looked at the house. Could he have had the nerve to have gone inside? He would have had to force his way in. She always kept it locked.

Kira decided to make a circuit of the house to look for a sign of entry. She was afraid, but she didn't know what else to do. Better she know the house was safe before she went inside.

She found the back door locked. Before continuing on around, she glanced out into the garden that had been her mother's pride and joy. The beds, which Irene Adamson had kept full of flowers, were mostly bare, though Kira had managed to keep up the shrubs and lawn.

As she surveyed the yard, her eyes were drawn to the ridge line of hills behind the house. There she saw him. He was standing on an outcropping of rock, perhaps two or three hundred yards away, looking down at her. She was too far from him to see his face, but his silhouette was outlined against the evening sky. He was motionless, his legs spread slightly, his arms at his side, his gaze appearing to be directed toward her.

For a long time Kira stared, wondering what he intended, if the strange moment implied danger. Why was he watching her that way?

She didn't wait to find out. Her father's shotgun was in the front hall closet, and there were some shells on the shelf. She would get Toby inside, then wait for Joshua Bearclaw to come to her, to make his intentions clear.

She considered calling the sheriff as a precaution. Bearclaw *was* trespassing. She had cause, but decided against it. No sense inflaming the situation unnecessarily.

She turned and walked quickly around the house. Even if he ran down the hill as fast as he could, she would have time to get Toby inside. But the imagined danger was too much for her to hold back. By the time she rounded the corner of the house, she was headed for the Jeep at a full run.

Toby saw her coming, scooted over and opened the door. "Thank you, honey," she said breathlessly, jumping into the seat. She fumbled to get the key in the ignition.

"Is he here?" Toby asked.

"There's a man on the hill. I think it might be him." The engine turned over several times before it finally caught. Her adrenaline was flowing, and she had to fight back the urge to panic. There's plenty of time, she told herself.

Jamming the car in gear, she stepped on the accelerator. The tires spun, kicking gravel up under the fenders. But the Jeep lurched ahead, and they quickly traversed the distance to the house.

"Jump out," she commanded, setting the hand brake and killing the engine. Kira got out herself and hurried around the vehicle. Toby was stepping down as she arrived at the passenger side.

"What about the food, Mom?"

"Never mind that now," she said, taking him by the arm. "We've got to get inside."

They mounted the steps, and Kira fumbled with the door key, trying to force herself to be calm. He hasn't done anything yet, she told herself, so don't panic. When the door was finally open, she shepherded her son inside. Then she locked and bolted the door behind them.

"Go to your room, Toby, and wait there."

"What's the matter?" he moaned, having fully picked up on her fear. "Is he going to hurt us?"

"No, honey. Everything's going to be fine. It's just that until I've talked to him, we've got to be careful. Don't turn on your lights, though. Get on your bed and listen to your tapes, okay?" She went to the hall closet.

"Mom," Toby lamented, "I want to stay with you."

She had taken her father's shotgun from the back of the closet and was searching for the box of shells. When she found it, she removed two. Breaking the gun, she inserted the cartridges into the breech. "All right, but be very quiet. Please."

Kira hadn't been a hunter like her father, but he'd shown her how to use a shotgun when she was still a girl. Until now, the knowledge had never been applied, but she was glad she at least knew what to do. With the gun hanging broken over her forearm, she made her way to the back of the house. Looking out the kitchen window, she saw him on the hillside. He was about halfway down, moving at a steady, but not a particularly hurried, pace.

Toby came up beside her and looked out the window.

"Is that him, my Indian father?"

"I think so."

They watched in silence for a moment.

"He doesn't have a gun," the boy said. "Are you going to shoot him anyway?"

"No, honey. Of course not."

"Then why do you have Grandpa's gun?"

"Because strangers aren't supposed to come onto your land uninvited. And if they do, you have to be prepared. There aren't any policemen around the corner, like in San Diego." Her comment made her think again of Conrad Willoughby's advice to call the sheriff if there was trouble. She weighed the possibility once more, but with the added security of the weapon, she decided against it again.

Kira's father had taught her that a shotgun should never be used in close quarters. She knew that meant the place to confront anyone would be outside, where they would be at a distance. She returned to the front room. Though leaving the security of the house didn't appeal to her, neither did talking to him through the door.

She turned to her son. "I'm going outside to talk to him, and I want you to stay here. I'm sure everything will be all right. But if there's trouble, you know how to call the sheriff."

Toby screwed up his face. "I don't want you to go, Mommy."

"It'll be fine, honey. You just do as I say." Kira knew Bearclaw would be arriving at any minute, so she opened the door and went onto the porch.

The sky had lost most of its color, and the evening had progressed into twilight. Overhead it was still fairly light, but the shadows under the trees were dark. She knew Toby would be listening and watching. Until Bearclaw demonstrated a hostile motive, she would give him the benefit of the doubt. She would talk to him, make it clear that his presence was unwanted.

Kira went down the steps and around the Jeep. Bearclaw's car was off to one side, and she moved well beyond it. She decided to meet him away from the house, where Toby couldn't easily overhear their conversation.

The shotgun was heavy, so Kira let it hang from one hand, still broken. She faced the hill behind the house, figuring he'd come through the trees just to the north. She waited and watched. There was neither sound nor motion.

The air had cooled considerably. She shivered. She hadn't thought to put on a jacket, and now she wished that she had. But it was too late. He'd had plenty of time to come the distance from where she'd last seen him.

Then, in the trees, she caught a flicker of motion. She lifted the shotgun, letting the barrel hang over her forearm as her father had taught her those long years ago. There was more motion in the shadows, then she saw a figure moving at a slow but deliberate pace in her direction. Her right hand tightened on the grip behind the trigger guard.

Two

The man appeared at the edge of the wood. He had stopped in the shadows, but Kira could see him. He was tall and well built. He wore jeans and boots and a leather jacket. He was bareheaded, though she couldn't see his expression.

"Mr. Bearclaw?" she said. She tried to sound forceful, but there was a faint tremor in her voice.

He started forward, and Kira snapped the breech of the gun closed. The man stopped dead in his tracks.

"The Navaho are a peaceful people now, Mrs. Lowell," he said in a clear voice. "We don't take scalps."

"You come where you aren't welcome. I don't appreciate that." He was perhaps fifty feet away. Kira kept the muzzle of the barrel pointed at the ground but in his general direction, to make her intentions clear.

"I've come to see my son."

"I thought I'd made it pretty clear that's not a good idea. Not now, anyway."

"You obviously weren't seeing it from my perspective," he said.

"I'm sympathetic with your request," she replied, "but I've got to be concerned with Toby's welfare."

"I am his father," Bearclaw said, his tone clear and forceful.

"You gave him life, but my husband and I raised him as our own. We are the only parents he has known."

"He is of my blood, Mrs. Lowell."

"He is my son, Mr. Bearclaw."

He started forward. Kira raised the muzzle, stopping him.

"Is this the way you talk?" he said, gesturing toward the gun.

The man was now enough in the open so that she could see his face. Black hair hung to his collar. His features were handsome, chiseled hawklike on his angular face. Bearclaw's cheekbones were high, his mouth thin and wide, his nose narrow, strong. Neither his features nor his physique seemed particularly like the Navaho, who were generally shorter and more rounded in both feature and build.

Kira and Dan had only seen Toby's mother once, at the time the adoption was being arranged. She was petite, with a pretty round face, large black eyes and lashes. Toby had his mother's eyes, but his finer features obviously came from his father's side. Kira could see the proof of that now.

"I mean you no harm," she said, "but you've come uninvited onto my land."

"I've only come to see my son. A man has a right to see his child. Whatever the laws, it's the way of nature." He started toward her again, so Kira pointed the weapon directly at his midsection.

"Stop there, Mr. Bearclaw. There's no need to come any closer." She looked at his face, hauntingly solemn in the muted twilight. His eyes were very pale, not dark like Toby's. They looked either blue or gray; he wasn't close enough for her to tell. And his skin was somewhat lighter than her son's, too. He looked as though he might have some white blood in him.

"Do you plan to shoot me?"

"I'm letting you know you can't come on my ranch and disregard my wishes. You said in your letters you're a lawyer. I must say, you don't act like one—claiming natural rights over the law."

"I didn't come to debate legal philosophy, Mrs. Lowell. I am a human being, with the same desires and instincts as any other person. The law is your law. I found it useful to study because there are so many more of you than there are of us. That's all."

"This has nothing to do with race. It simply has to do with a child's welfare."

"I, too, am concerned about my son. I worry that he is being raised in ignorance of his heritage, his people, his blood."

"Toby is a human being...like you and me and everyone else on this planet."

Bearclaw paused, his pale eyes glowing in the subdued light. "The boy is an Indian."

The words were pronounced with such gravity that Kira felt herself tremble from the power of his presence. There was neither hatred nor anger in his eyes—merely the forceful expression of will. She didn't answer for a moment; she simply stared at the haunting, brooding face that struck her as almost beautiful for its majesty. "I don't accept that," she finally murmured.

"You cannot change it," Bearclaw replied. "The boy is what he is."

Kira drew a deep breath, withdrawing herself forcefully from the man's spell. "You don't know what Toby is. But I do."

"Then as his father, I want to know him, too. Is that unreasonable by any standard?"

His intractable nature began to frustrate her, and Kira felt the tension building. "Let's be honest," she snapped, unintentionally waving the muzzle of the gun. "Your intention isn't to get to know Toby. You want him. You want to take him from me."

Bearclaw shook his head. "That is your fear speaking, not my words. I only want to know my son and for him to know me. Through me he will know his culture, his people and his blood."

"Those are nice words, Mr. Bearclaw, but what do they really mean? Has it occurred to you that Toby might already have a satisfying identity? That he has a mother who loves him, and a home?"

"If your child, one you gave birth to, lived with me on the reservation, would you say the same? If he had fair skin and light hair and grew up without hamburgers and Little League baseball and Sunday school because his Indian parents showed him their way, not yours, would you feel the same? Would you not hunger for him to have a glimpse of your world, just to know it existed?"

Kira looked into his eyes, alive with the fire of his words. His tremulous voice, his heart-piercing beauty weakened her, distracted her from the logic of her own position. "You are asking for my child," she whispered.

"I want him not to wonder when he looks at his school picture and sees all those white faces around his. I want him to know where he came from and to feel pride and peace about his ancestors. My son might love you, Mrs. Lowell. He might love you as he can never learn to love me. But he will always know that he is not of your people. This will weigh on him more than the fact that he is not of your body."

Kira shook her head. "You don't know that. You fear it, or wish it so, I'm not sure which. Even if you are right, Mr. Bearclaw, life will give Toby plenty of opportunity to decide for himself."

"No. So long as you make him something he is not, he will only suffer into adulthood, wondering and doubting."

She could see the man would not give up until the law placed insurmountable obstacles in his way, or until she shot him. Neither course would be pleasant. She remembered Conrad Willoughby's advice to find a way to work things out and wondered if making some sort of concession would really be as bad for her son as she had imagined.

"What would you like, exactly? To meet Toby and talk to him about your people?"

"Yes."

"Is that all?"

"To know him and have him know me, if he will."

"And how long do you envision this taking? One visit? Two?"

"I'm an ordinary man, Mrs. Lowell, not a medicine man or a psychiatrist. And the boy is not a dog to be trained. I am who I am. He is who he is. We have in common our blood. Beyond that, I can't say."

Kira had let the shotgun sag. Bearclaw was less than twenty feet away. They were both growing obscure in fading light. The air was becoming cooler, and she trembled with the cold. But his countenance was still having its effect on her. Whether it was force of personality or some sort of intangible spirituality, she wasn't sure. But it frightened her, yet drew her to him at the same time.

As they looked into each other's eyes, Bearclaw's dream and Toby's future hung in the balance. The silence was broken by the distant sound of a vehicle. Bearclaw turned, as Kira did, toward the place where the driveway disappeared over the edge of the bluff. Nothing could be seen initially, then, as headlights swept through the opaque air of evening, Kira remembered that Rod Banyon was coming to dinner.

She glanced at Joshua Bearclaw, who continued staring down the driveway. Then he slowly shifted his eyes toward her. They seemed luminous, as though a light was coming from within them. His eyes fascinated her, and she wanted to ask him about them, but Rod's arrival would prevent it.

"You expecting someone?" he asked, tossing his head toward the western sky.

"Yes. A friend is coming to dinner."

As she spoke, Rod's Corvette appeared over the crest of the bluff, the beams from the headlights falling directly on them. Kira lowered the shotgun, realizing what a shock it would be for Rod to find her with a gun trained on a strange man.

In seconds the car slid to a halt. Though the headlights were bright, she could see the car door open and Rod's lanky body uncoil as he climbed out. His silhouette was barely visible against the dying color of the sky.

"Kira? What's going on?" He moved toward her without bothering to close the door, looking back and forth between her and Bearclaw. He nodded toward the gun. "Trouble?" he said, his tone more conclusive than inquiring.

"It's all right, Rod. We were just talking."

"With a twenty-gauge?"

"This is Joshua Bearclaw, Toby's natural father." She turned, gesturing toward the man at her side. "My friend, Rod Banyon, Mr. Bearclaw."

The businessman eyed the man who, like them, was bathed in the headlights of the Corvette. "You're Indian, then."

"I'm Navaho, Mr. Banyon."

"What are you doing clear up here in Oregon?"

"I came to see my son."

Rod looked at Kira. "That what the shotgun's all about? You trying to run him off? He bothering you?" He looked at Bearclaw, his expression hardening.

"No," Kira said. "I wasn't sure of his intentions, or even who he was when I first saw him. I brought Dad's gun as a precaution."

Rod's eyes narrowed. "Didn't anybody ever teach you to call before you drop in?"

"I wrote, instead. Not the best Emily Post, maybe, but I'd hoped it'd do."

"This guy being smart, or what?"

Kira could see that Banyon had his dander up.

"You being smart, buddy?" He squared his shoulders.

Rod had played football at Seneca Falls High, and Kira knew he had played some at Oregon State before injuring his knee. He wasn't a small man, nor did he lack for courage. But one look told her Bearclaw wasn't intimidated. There would be trouble if she didn't put a stop to this. Kira took Rod's arm. "Please, this is my business. I can handle it."

Banyon shifted his weight from foot to foot, like a prizefighter trying to deal with his adrenaline before a bout. His hands moved to his hips. "Well, we going to stand out here and chat in the dark, or invite Emily Post here in for tea?"

Kira glanced at Bearclaw, but he was looking beyond them, toward the house. His luminescent eyes had widened, and there was wonder in them. She turned back and saw what had captured his attention. Toby was walking toward them, having traversed about half the distance from the house. Rod looked back, too.

"Mom," the boy said, "I'm getting hungry. Aren't we going to eat?"

"Toby..." She started to send him back—to admonish him for coming out of the house against her orders—but he had to have been terribly curious. And with Rod there, he had undoubtedly judged it safe.

The boy hurried to her side, wrapping his arm around her waist. He was staring at his father. Kira brushed back his hair and looked up at Bearclaw.

He was gazing intently at his child, his eyes fairly dancing. She couldn't be sure if it was delight or awe. There was a long silence in which Rod Banyon, like she, watched the two of them.

"Hello, little brother," Bearclaw finally said.

Kira felt the boy squirm against her leg. He looked up at her. "I thought you said he was my father," he said in a tiny voice.

Bearclaw laughed. It was a deep joyful sound. Then he smiled, his white teeth showing in the automobile's lights. It was the first time his expression had changed since she had laid eyes on him. There was such happiness on his face that she felt herself smiling, too.

"It is an expression of our people," Bearclaw said. "The Navaho are like one family, one body. You are my brother, as well as my son."

Kira felt the child's fingers digging into her leg. "Mom, is that true?" he whispered.

"It is the Indian belief," she said.

Toby looked at his father again.

"Mrs. Lowell," Bearclaw said, "will you permit me to shake hands with my little brother?"

Kira glanced at the boy, then at Rod. Toby looked up at her questioningly, as if to ask if it was what he should do. She felt her stomach clench. "Would you like to say hello to him, honey?"

Toby gave a little nod. "I guess so."

She put her hand on his shoulder and squeezed it tightly, holding on to him as though she were fearful he might fly away. He looked into her eyes. She nodded, then released him.

Toby took a couple of hesitant steps forward. When Bearclaw extended his open palm and dropped to one knee, Toby clasped his fingers. Then the man rested his hand on the child's shoulder.

Kira couldn't see Toby's face, but she saw Bearclaw's eyes moisten, shimmering in the headlights of the Corvette. "It's good to be with you," she heard him say. "I hope one day we will know each other as true brothers."

Toby didn't say anything, nor did he move. Kira wondered if he was as transfixed by the man's eyes as she. Bearclaw touched his son's cheek, then let his hand drop. After a moment the child turned around and marched back to her.

"Rod," she said, "would you mind taking Toby inside? I want to conclude my conversation with Mr. Bearclaw."

"You sure, Kira?"

"Yes, I'll be fine. Please take him in the house."

"If you're sure." He went back to his car and extinguished the headlights, plunging the area into a darkness lighted only by the night sky. Rod slammed the car door and returned to her. He hesitated, and she handed him the shotgun.

He looked at her uncertainly, then took the boy's hand, and they slowly walked toward the house. Kira took a few steps toward Bearclaw, then stopped. There was something about him that made her afraid, even though he was thoroughly fascinating.

"That won't satisfy you, will it?" she said.

"No, Mrs. Lowell."

"To be honest, I don't know what to do," she said with a sigh. "I think I want to sleep on it. But I'll talk to you tomorrow, and we'll see if we can come to some kind of arrangement."

Bearclaw smiled for a second time. A silvery light from behind her was falling on his face, adding drama to his features. Standing closer, she could see that his eyes were gray, with a dark ring around the iris. They were the most unusual eyes she had ever seen.

It was very cold, and she began to tremble. She hugged herself, rubbing her arms. "Can you come back tomorrow afternoon?" she asked. "Say about two o'clock?"

He nodded, his formidable will harnessed, restrained.

"Don't ask for too much," she warned. "This is terribly difficult for me. Terribly difficult."

Bearclaw elevated his chin, drawing a deep breath. "I know." Then he stepped to her, lifted his hands slowly and took the ends of her shoulders in his large warm palms. He stared straight into her eyes. "You are both wise and generous, Mrs. Lowell. The gift you have given me is very great, indeed."

His eyes seemed to shimmer. Then Joshua Bearclaw leaned forward and kissed her on the forehead. The gesture was compassionate, priestlike. "That's not an Indian custom," he said softly, the faintest smile touching his lips. "It's merely the gratitude of a happy man."

He walked past her to where the car was parked. Kira turned to watch him. She was shivering violently, but she wasn't sure if it was because of the cold or him.

He started his car and began driving away. She stared after the vehicle until it was completely out of sight. Then she headed for the house.

Above the rooftop, she saw the moon rising over the mountain to the east. She had seen the sight many times, but its beauty was enough to make her stop for a moment. Behind her, the sound of Bearclaw's car was fading. A breeze picked up, carrying the chilly air down the slope of the mountain.

For some reason, Kira didn't want to go inside. She turned, instead, and looked at the purplish black of the western sky, facing the direction Joshua Bearclaw had disappeared.

Three

_____

Kira spent the next morning anxiously waiting for Joshua Bearclaw's arrival. She had been so thoroughly fascinated the previous evening that she was as eager as she was apprehensive. His eyes, the mood he had evoked in the twilight, had haunted her. Even during dinner, she found herself thinking about him, Rod Banyon notwithstanding.

After Toby had gone to bed, Rod and Kira sat in the front room, listening to records on the stereo and talking. She was only half listening to Rod's discourse about some business he was planning on buying. Even when he kissed her, she was only partially aware of his presence. She was thinking about Joshua Bearclaw.

But when Rod got more aggressive, caressing her breast, she put a stop to his advances.

"What's the matter?" he had asked with annoyance. "Don't you like me kissing and loving you?"

"Well, I am . . . fond of you, Rod," she had said. "I'm distracted, that's all."

"By what? That Indian?"

"I'm worried about Toby."

"The solution to that's easy enough. Don't let the guy come on the place. If he gets insistent, send some bird shot over his shoulder. He'll think twice."

"I can't blame him for wanting to see his son."

Rod Banyon had looked at her then in a way that made her feel guilty. "If you aren't up to handling him, Kira, I'll see to it for you."

"Thanks," she said, touching her finger to the corner of his mouth, "but I can take care of it."

Rod had wanted things to get more romantic then, but she wasn't interested. It took stubborn insistence and some diplomacy, but he finally left without things getting intimate. It was fairly obvious Rod felt it was time they start sleeping together.

But Kira hardly gave Rod Banyon another thought. Toby and Joshua Bearclaw were on her mind when she climbed into bed, and they were on her mind the minute she woke up. Though she had no specific recollection, she was sure she must have dreamed about Joshua half the night.

He was coming in only a few hours, and Kira hadn't yet decided what she would tell him. At first, she thought that he shouldn't see the boy again, then she concluded it wouldn't be so bad—so long as it involved just one or two brief visits. But would that satisfy him? Perhaps it was better not to get started at all. Kira spent the day vacillating. By the time two o'clock came, she was emotionally exhausted.

When Bearclaw's rental car appeared over the edge of the bluff, she was at the window. He parked where he had the night before, and she watched as he got out of the vehicle and walked toward the house.

In broad daylight he looked less spiritual and more conventionally handsome, though there was an aura about him that was different than any man she had ever known. She wasn't sure if it was his looks, his demeanor or what. He was dressed pretty much the same as the previous night, though he didn't have on the leather jacket. Instead he wore a clean, neatly pressed blue work shirt with epaulets, the sleeves rolled up to the middle of his arms. As he mounted the steps, Kira went to the door.

There was a half smile on his face as she greeted him. He wore a somewhat expectant expression, though there was a serenity about him that pervaded everything. But it was his strange wonderful eyes that attracted her greatest attention. She only managed words of welcome before she was entranced by them.

"Right on time, Mr. Bearclaw." She stepped back to admit him to the house.

He looked around, seemingly curious. It was evident he was evaluating the place. He turned to her. "Nice home."

"It was my parents' place. They were killed in an accident a year ago this coming winter. My things—our things—are in storage for the most part."

Bearclaw was studying her. His intensity unnerved her, and she felt uncomfortable. She gestured toward the couch.

"Won't you sit down?"

He sat in an armchair. Kira sat opposite him on the couch.

"You've suffered some tragedies," he said simply.

"You know about my husband."

"I'm aware you're a widow."

The way he said it made Kira feel vulnerable. She drew herself up. "Dan was a flight instructor in the navy. Five years ago he was demonstrating an approach to stalls, was unable to recover and crashed. It was a freak thing, a combination of misjudgment and equipment failure."

"I'm sorry."

"Last year my parents were killed. So, yes, I guess I've had my share of tragedy."

Bearclaw was sitting still, as though he were measuring her, judging her. His eyes didn't quit her face. "Was my son close to your husband?"

"Toby loved Dan. They were close, yes."

He made no comment.

"Does it make any difference to you that I'm raising him alone?" Kira asked.

"The influence of a man is important. But I'm not so concerned with that as I am with his life generally."

"I hope you've seen enough to realize that Toby is in a wholesome environment, and that he's happy."

"You seem like a decent woman, Mrs. Lowell. But to know Toby's life, I must know him."

Kira felt threatened by the words, though there was nothing hostile in Bearclaw's tone. She looked for signs of menace, but all she saw was his mysterious intriguing countenance. "So, we come to the purpose of your visit."

"You did say you'd give me an answer to my request."

She swallowed hard, feeling trapped and helpless, yet at the same time ready to spring into combat with this man who threatened the life she'd built. "To be honest, Mr. Bearclaw, I haven't decided what to do."

"What are your doubts?"

Kira fidgeted uncomfortably. "I guess I'm suspicious of your motives."

"I've explained them as best I can. I don't know what else I can say to reassure you."

"Maybe it's you, then. You've come here out of the blue, and I don't even know who you are."

"What do you want to know?"

"Tell me about yourself—where you came from, what you're doing, where you're headed."

He smiled wryly. "I should have brought you a résumé."

"I want to know about the man who wants to know my son."

"The request is a fair one," he replied. "You know I had an affair with Toby's mother. It wasn't an important relationship, but it produced the child. I can't say I'm proud of this. She was very young. I was a man, and I should have been more responsible. But I hadn't found my heart, my place in this world. I was fighting life, instead of living it."

"What do you mean?"

"I was twenty-six when Toby was conceived. I had done nothing with my life. I drank too much. I fought for no good reason except to vent my anger. And I carry the scars of my wild living." He turned his head, revealing a thin white line along the side of his neck.

"What happened?"

"A fight with a Mexican. If his knife had gone half an inch farther, I'd be dead."

Kira gasped.

"I had nothing to be proud of, save my ability to fight men and seduce women. Neither brought me happiness. So I left the reservation, looking for fights of a different nature. Eventually I drifted into the struggle for Indian causes. For a while I worked with a public action group. With them I learned the secret of the white man's power. I learned that it was more important what you have in your head than in your fists."

"And so you are a lawyer."

"Yes, I finished law school last year. I hope to do some good for my people."

"What you've done is admirable."

"Mrs. Lowell, I want you to know that I am a decent man by the white man's standard, as well as that of my people."

"So I'm to conclude that it would be good for you to spend time with Toby."

"I hope that's what you will decide."

Kira drew a deep breath. Bearclaw was staring at her, quietly probing. She had no way to know about his skills as a fighter or even as a lawyer, but as a woman she understood his seductive powers. It was probably the furthest thing from his mind just then, but she felt his allure, understood how a woman could succumb to him.

"I like to think I'm a compassionate human being," Kira began. "I have a great deal of sympathy for your desire to know Toby. As a parent, your fervor moves me. But I could never do anything to hurt him."

"Nor could I, Mrs. Lowell."

"My perspective is a little different than yours. I will tell you, though, that Toby's reaction to you didn't distress me. He seemed to handle it okay."

Bearclaw waited calmly, listening. She could feel his intensity. "What is your decision?"

"You can stay until Toby comes home from school. Then you can spend some time with him. But if and when I decide the visit should end, you'll have to leave."

He broke into a broad grin, looking very happy. "Thank you."

Kira was warmed by his gratitude. She knew the decision would please him, but a part of her still doubted it was the wise thing to do. She hoped she hadn't let his unusual charm, his allure, warp her reasoning. His remark about his seductive powers went through her mind again as she looked at her watch. "Well, we have some time before Toby'll be getting home from school. Would you like to see his room? Then maybe we can have a cup of coffee."

"I'd like both."

She led him into the small bedroom she'd had as a girl. The furniture was feminine, but Kira explained the reason, noting they'd managed to cover it up some with the traditional boyish touches.

Bearclaw noticed the poster of the San Diego Padres on the wall. He went to the dresser and looked at the trinkets Toby kept on its top: a key ring, a couple of marbles, a balsa wood glider, a small box full of rubber bands, a bird feather. Then he picked up the framed photograph of Dan Lowell in a flight suit, standing in front of a fighter plane.

"Your husband looked like a kind man," the Indian said without turning around. "He had a friendly face."

"Dan was kind," Kira said, her voice betraying the slightest tremor. "And he loved Toby."

"I would like to have met him."

"I'm sorry you can't."

Then Bearclaw turned to face her, his white-hot eyes luminous the way they had been in the twilight the evening before. "What about Rod Banyon? Is he your lover?"

Kira was indignant at first, until she realized he wasn't prying. He was thinking of his son—the degree to which Toby and Rod might become involved because of her relationship. "He and I are friends."

"I think your friend is a jealous man and wishes to be more than just your friend."

Again she was surprised, both by his audacity and the accuracy of the insight. "What makes you so sure?"

"I saw the way he looked at you, Mrs. Lowell. I saw the way he looked at me."

"You're very perceptive." She hesitated, then pushed on. "Do Rod's feelings toward me bother you?"

"You're a beautiful woman. I suspect there are many men who would want to marry you. That means one could become the father of my son. It's something for me to think about."

"You didn't answer my question."

"Rod Banyon doesn't like me. My feelings toward him are the same." His gaze skittered down her body before he turned to examine a small shelf of books on the wall.

The look he'd given her was the first overt sign of regard he had made. Even the kiss the night before was one of human compassion, not one motivated by sexual awareness.

Kira noted his broad shoulders and coal-black hair hanging to his shirt collar. His waist was trim, his body hard, athletic. He was quite appealing, and the fact that he was an Indian struck her as romantic instead of frightening, as it had seemed in his letters. But she quickly brushed the thought aside.

"I hope that because of Toby, you won't feel the need to take a personal interest in every man who comes into my life."

There was a grin on his face as he turned around. "We are bound together in a way, you and I, aren't we?"

"I don't see that we're bound together at all, Mr. Bearclaw. You're only here at my indulgence. As a lawyer, you must be aware that I can keep you away from Toby very easily, if I choose."

He shook his head. "As a lawyer, I am aware that my little brother is with you only at the indulgence of the Navaho nation."

Her brow furrowed. "What are you talking about?"

"The Indian Child Welfare Act."

"The what?"

"Congress gave jurisdiction of all Indian children to the tribal courts, including decisions regarding custody. Any adoption of an Indian child without the sanction of the tribal courts is invalid."

"That's not true," Kira protested. "The California courts gave Toby to Dan and me, with his mother's permission. It was a legal adoption. Just because you're coming along after the fact, doesn't mean it's invalid."

"I said nothing about me, Mrs. Lowell. This is a tribal concern. I'm simply telling you that unless the tribe approves the adoption, it is not valid. Even a child's parents can't alienate him from the tribe without its concurrence."

Her eyes flashed. "I don't believe you."

"Check with your lawyer."

"I have. I talked with him today, as a matter of fact. He didn't say anything about any act of Congress. Neither did the lawyer who handled the adoption in San Diego."

"It's a specialized area of the law. It is unlikely a general practitioner here would have run into the issue. I don't know what the fellow's excuse was in San Diego."

"Well, I certainly intend to find out about this."

"I think it would be wise."

Kira's hands settled on her hips. "I knew this wasn't the innocent visit you made it out to be."

"Now wait a minute," he said, raising his hand. "I'm not threatening anything. I was simply informing you of something you obviously were ignorant of. The tribe's rights are unimportant, unless they choose to exercise them.''

She scoffed. ''I'm no fool, Mr. Bearclaw. Aren't you telling me that if you want to bring this to the tribe's attention, you can make trouble for me? Aren't you really holding it over my head? Assuming that it's true, of course.''

''I'm doing no such thing. I wasn't even sure that you were unaware of it, until you started pontificating about your rights.''

''Pontificating?'' Kira turned on her heel and walked from the room.

She was looking out the front window when Bearclaw came up behind her. She spun around. He was standing a few feet from her, looking distressed.

''Mrs. Lowell, please accept my apology. I was unkind. I shouldn't have said what I did.''

He seemed sincere, and her anger immediately dissipated. ''Is that business about the tribal courts really true?''

''Yes.''

''Have you discussed it with them? Do they know about Toby?''

He shook his head.

Kira turned to the window again. She wished her son would come over the edge of the bluff. She wished he was there. And she wished Joshua Bearclaw was gone. The thought of sending him away crossed her mind momentarily, but she decided against it. There was no point in provoking him, though she still had her doubts about this act of Congress he alluded to.

She faced him then, gathering herself in an attempt to be pleasant. ''How about that cup of coffee? I think I have some cookies, too, if Toby hasn't eaten them all.'' She gave a halfhearted laugh and walked past him toward the kitchen. "Sit down and make yourself at home," she said over her shoulder. "I'll serve the coffee in here."

As Kira put the water on to boil, she tried to figure out the implications of Joshua Bearclaw's news. Despite his denial, she was sure he intended to use the threat of tribal intervention against her. How could he not? After all, what did she mean to him? If he wanted Toby, he would undoubtedly use whatever resources were at his disposal.

But if that was the case, why bother with her at all? He could have gotten the tribal court after her from the beginning.

Kira paced back and forth. What was Bearclaw up to? Could he *really* have Toby's welfare at heart? Maybe he genuinely wanted to assure himself that his son was in a good home with a loving mother. Maybe seeing that, he would go away satisfied. Or was that ridiculously naive?

In any case, Kira saw no point in alienating the man unnecessarily. If he was honorable and decent, it was better to have him as a friend. How ironic, she decided, that he came to her beholding—or so she thought—when maybe he was the one with the whip hand.

"You okay?"

She gasped at the voice behind her and spun around. Bearclaw was leaning against the doorjamb, watching her. "I wish you wouldn't sneak up on me like that. You scared me to death."

"Didn't know that I was. Sorry."

He smiled, and for the second time, Kira was cognizant of an awareness on his part. His look said he was seeing her as a woman. She felt for the counter behind her, keeping her eyes on him, feeling fear again.

"I was sitting in there, thinking about you," he said, "and it occurred to me you might be feeling rather insecure. I know I would be in your shoes. I just wanted to re-assure you."

"You're very thoughtful," she replied. "And percep-tive."

"My intentions are good. I've been honest with you."

"Yes, you've said that." There was a touch of skepti-cism in her voice.

"And I take it the best way for me to prove it," he said wryly, "would be to ride off into the sunset."

"In spite of our problems, Toby and I have a very happy life. I'd hate for something to upset it."

"Or someone?"

"Yes, or someone."

"I like you, Mrs. Lowell. That ought to give you some assurance."

Kira smiled tentatively. The kettle began to sing. She poured some water into a couple of mugs on the counter. "Hope you don't mind instant." When she turned around, a mug in each hand, he was staring at her intently. He had said he liked her, but she sensed more in his wondrous mysterious eyes than that. "There's a plate of cookies," she said, trying to cover her befuddlement. "Would you mind bringing them in?"

Despite his boots, he managed to walk behind her in near silence as they made their way into the front room. She was acutely aware of him, imagining that he was looking at her body, perhaps thinking of her in sexual terms. As they sat down, she even wondered if he might try to take advantage of her.

She leaned across the small coffee table, holding out the plate of cookies he'd put down. He took one, thanking her. For several minutes they drank their coffee and munched on cookies, their eyes frequently meeting before Kira looked away.

"I wish I hadn't told you about the Indian Child Welfare Act," he said after a while. "It's made you distrustful."

"You think I trusted you before?" She smiled.

"You were confident because you thought you had the upper hand."

"Your insight is remarkable," she said, "but not so remarkable as your willingness to share your observations."

"I'm plainspoken and it offends you." There was a touch of humor in his voice, and he smiled slightly. His mystery was slowly giving way to his charm.

"You said, or implied, that you'd given up fighting. Have you given up seducing women, as well?"

"We're both plainspoken, I see," he said with a laugh. He took a bite of cookie, his eyes dancing as they bored into her.

Kira met his gaze until she couldn't hold it any longer. "You didn't answer my question," she said, taking a cookie to cover her embarrassment.

"My character and qualifications as a parent are not at issue," he replied.

"Are mine?"

"Frankly, yes, Mrs. Lowell."

She looked away, stung by his remark. But on reflection she realized he was just speaking the truth. His style was simply a little more forthright than most.

"Tell me about your parentage," she said. "You're not a full-blooded Indian, are you?"

"I am three-quarters Navaho. My mother's father was a white man. I don't know much about him—he was gone, perhaps dead, before I was born. They say he was very tall and had light gray eyes, like the sky."

"That's where you got yours."

"My friends, when I was a boy, said it was from the wolves."

"Are you sure that wasn't what the girls said?"

Bearclaw sipped his coffee, hiding his smile behind the rim of the cup.

Another flicker of embarrassment went through her. "I'm as interested in knowing the father of my son as you are in knowing about me," she said by way of explanation, "though for different reasons."

"You want to know where he came from, and I want to know where he is now."

"Yes, that's probably the best way to describe it."

"It's as I said earlier, we are bound together by the boy. There is no escaping the fact."

They heard the sound of footsteps and then running feet on the porch. The front door opened and Toby burst in, coming to a sudden stop, his eyes round as he stared at them. Bearclaw stood.

"Well, little brother, you've come home. Hello."

Toby's voice was small. "Hello."

"We're having some cookies," Kira said. "Would you like to get yourself a glass of milk and join us?"

Toby nodded.

"Put your books in your room and come along, then."

She watched Bearclaw as the boy walked across the room. He wore the same expression of delight he'd shown the night before. His eyes were glistening when he turned back to her.

"This is a joy, Mrs. Lowell."

Kira had to swallow the lump in her throat. Their jousting paled alongside the humanity of the moment.

The child joined them with a glass of milk, sitting on the couch, close to his mother. The three of them chatted for a while, the boy gradually warming to the man. At one point Toby jumped up and ran to his room to get a book on the Navaho that she had given him for Christmas the year before.

"Yes," Bearclaw said, looking through it, "I saw this on your shelf."

"Is that the way it is where we come from?"

"It's romanticized a bit, but it's not an unfair picture."

"Do you live that way?" Toby asked.

"The house I live in now is not a hogan. It's made of cement blocks, and I have electricity, but the culture of our people is still alive."

"What's 'culture'?"

Bearclaw laughed. "Ah, there is so much for you to learn." Then he turned to Kira. "Would it be all right if Toby and I went for a walk?"

She glanced at the boy. Toby wore an expectant expression. "If he wants to, it's okay with me," she replied.

"What do you say, little brother?"

Toby nodded enthusiastically. "Yeah, it's okay with me."

Bearclaw and the boy went out of the house. Kira watched them head for the small wood. She figured they would climb the hill behind the house. As soon as they were gone, she went to the telephone in the kitchen and called Conrad Willoughby.

When she'd explained what Joshua Bearclaw had said, he told her he'd have to do some research to assess the implications of any such act of Congress, but that he'd get her a general answer whether the law even existed after he'd had a chance to call the law library at the courthouse.

Kira hung up, then paced around the house, going to the back window to watch for a sign of them while she waited. She didn't see what Bearclaw had to gain by lying, but she wanted to hear it from someone she trusted. After a while, she saw them working their way up the hillside, headed for the outcropping of rock where she had spotted Bearclaw the previous evening.

Finally they reached the spot and stood just as Bearclaw had, looking out over the valley. She saw him gesturing broadly and wondered what he could be saying. Perhaps he was telling Toby the Indian story of creation, or just making an observation that before the white man all the land belonged to the Indians, along with the antelope and the buffalo.

As she watched, Bearclaw put his hand on the boy's shoulder. Seeing them together, Kira wondered if she hadn't made a mistake. But the phone rang, interrupting her musings. It was Conrad Willoughby.

"I'm going to look into this in detail," the lawyer said, "but I wanted you to know that the act of Congress Bearclaw mentioned does exist, and it does give jurisdiction over Indian children exclusively to the tribal courts."

"Does that mean they can take Toby from me?"

"I don't know yet, honey. That's something I'll have to check into."

A sinking feeling came over her as she hung up. Kira returned to the window expectantly, hoping to see her son, but Bearclaw and Toby had disappeared.

Four

Kira sat on the front porch, watching Bearclaw's car, waiting for them to return from their father-and-son walk. Conrad Willoughby's news had left her with a feeling of dread, though she hadn't really doubted the Indian's story. But now her vulnerability was undeniable. She thought of Dan Lowell and the joy they'd shared when Toby had first come into their lives. Her eyes filled with tears. Why did Dan have to die and leave her to face the world alone?

Kira had let herself get into a morose state by the time she heard Toby and Bearclaw coming through the wood. She got to her feet as the boy ran toward her at full tilt.

"Mom, Mom, guess what?" He came up to her breathlessly, a happy smile on his face.

"What, Toby?"

He gestured over his shoulder. "He brought me a present. Something sacred."

"What sort of present?"

"I don't know. He said it's in the car. He's going to give it to me."

She glanced at Bearclaw, who was opening the trunk. Toby ran to him and returned a moment later with a bundle of some sort in his arms. It was a rug or blanket, neatly folded. He carried it very solemnly.

"What is it, honey?"

"An Indian rug, Mom. He said my great-grandmother made it. It's sacred." There was awe on Toby's face as he looked down at the bundle.

Bearclaw came up behind the boy. "I thought he might like a little something to go on his wall along with the Padres."

"That's very thoughtful," Kira said. "I'm sure he'll treasure it."

They went inside and Bearclaw helped the youngster unfold the rug. Then he explained the various markings and designs. Toby listened with rapt attention.

Kira listened, too, but she was really watching the man. Bearclaw's intensity and force of personality seemed overwhelming, and she felt weak at the thought of having to fight him for her son. And Toby appeared as mesmerized as she. He sat on his heels, listening to his father's every word. She wondered if she'd already lost him.

When Bearclaw finished his discourse, he and the boy folded the rug and Toby took it to his room, carrying it as though it were already his most treasured possession. Bearclaw turned to her, smiling happily.

"He is a wonderful boy, Mrs. Lowell."

Kira nodded sadly.

"Today is one of the happiest days of my life," he said.

"It's an important one for Toby, too, I'm sure."

"You've been most generous. You're a good woman."

In his eyes, Kira saw more than gratitude and happiness. His look was saying something to her, something his lips hadn't uttered. They stared at each other in silence until Toby returned.

"When can we hang my rug, Mom? I want to put it up so that I can see it."

"We'll do it soon. Maybe tomorrow morning, or tonight after dinner, if there's time."

Toby plopped down next to her on the couch. She looked at Bearclaw. He was still studying her. She began to feel a bit uncomfortable.

"It's been a nice visit," she said, trying to fill the void. "It's meant a lot to Toby. I think, to both of you."

"I am grateful. And to show my gratitude, I'd like to take both of you to dinner."

"That's awfully nice, but there's no place near and—"

"We can drive into Seneca Falls, if you don't mind the time."

"Oh, Mom, could we?" the boy piped up. "We never get to eat out."

Kira laughed, tousling his hair. "Hey, young man, you're giving away all our family secrets."

"I would consider it an honor," Bearclaw said. "A small token of my thanks."

While Kira freshened up and changed, the man and boy played checkers in the front room. The happiness and contentment of the two had begun to rub off on her, and by the time she had dressed, her spirits were up again. Looking into her own green eyes in the mirror, she tried to see herself as Bearclaw saw her.

It was clear enough that she found him attractive, but she sensed an awareness on his part, too, and that bothered her because she didn't know what it meant. She was glad for Toby's sake that she liked Bearclaw and that he seemed fond of her, but she didn't want it to go any further than that. More could be dangerous.

It probably wasn't very smart to have agreed to go to dinner with him, but the invitation was innocent enough, and the final question remained unresolved. Where was Joshua Bearclaw willing to leave things? She didn't want to press matters because, with luck, he just might say his goodbyes and return to Arizona. It was her best hope.

Kira was smiling, determined to remain cheerful, when she returned to the front room. Seeing her, Bearclaw slowly got to his feet, his eyes moving up and down her body.

"Gee, Mom," Toby said, looking over his shoulder at her, "you got all dressed up."

"You mother is very beautiful, little brother," Bearclaw said. "You must be proud of her."

The boy glanced first at his father, then at her. He got up, too. "Aren't we going to finish our game?"

"If we're going all the way to Seneca Falls, we have to get going so you can get home before bedtime," Kira said.

"You're the checkers champion until next time," Bearclaw added.

His words were innocent on the surface, but they hinted at something she'd been fearing. Was the man seriously thinking in terms of other visits, or was it simply a meaningless remark?

They went out to Bearclaw's car, then drove off toward the highway as the sun set behind the ridge line across the valley. Toby sat in back, hanging over the seat between them. They chatted inconsequentially, mostly about the Navaho, Bearclaw answering the boy's questions.

But Kira was preoccupied. She thought about her husband again, using her memories as a kind of shield against the man she was with. She remembered when the three of them would go out in the evening. Dan liked taking them to the officers' club, because he was very proud of his family.

When they had been unable to have children and the doctors determined it was because of Dan's sterility, he had been depressed at the notion that Kira wouldn't be able to have children. He had suggested artificial insemination, but she hadn't wanted to bear a child unless it was his. Adoption seemed the ideal solution. And when the opportunity to get Toby came along, they were both overjoyed.

Kira glanced over at Bearclaw as he drove. With the fading light that special aura returned—one that seemed to come with the evening shadows. He was a magnetic man, and he affected her strongly. Coming on the heels of thoughts about her husband, she resented him for it.

By the time they arrived in Seneca Falls, she was confused again, not knowing what sort of attitude to have, not sure exactly how she felt. After a brief discussion about where to eat, they settled on Cattlemen's. Bearclaw drove to the restaurant. They pulled into the parking lot just at dusk.

Getting out of the car, Kira noticed Rod Banyon's black Corvette parked nearby. She didn't say anything, but a feeling of dread went through her.

Inside, to her relief, she didn't spot Rod. The hostess seated them inconspicuously in a corner of the dining room. A few people looked their way, and Kira could tell there were comments about them at other tables. It would have happened to any local in the company of a stranger, but she sensed a particular curiosity because Bearclaw was an Indian.

Kira wondered if Toby was aware of the gossip, but there was no sign that he was. The waitress had taken their orders, and he was telling his father about school, when a presence loomed at Kira's side. It was Rod Banyon, a glass of beer in his hand.

"I was in the bar and heard you'd come in," he said. "Would I be interrupting the happy little family if I joined you?"

She glanced at Bearclaw, who was looking up at Rod with a steady gaze. The tension was almost palpable. She knew she had to act quickly. "Sit down, if you like, Rod," she said, gesturing toward the empty chair between her and Toby.

He sat, tousling the boy's hair as he did. "How you doing, sonny?"

Toby hardly looked at the man. "Okay."

Nobody said anything for several moments. Rod took a long drink, then turned to the others. "Well, let's not sit here like a bunch of cigar-store Indians." Then he laughed, drunkenly.

Bearclaw's expression hardened. "I don't mind you making a joke at my expense, Mr. Banyon," he said, "but let's take it easy with the boy."

Rod blinked with surprise. "What?" Then a grin crept across his face. "Oh, I didn't mean anything. We're always kidding around, aren't we, sonny?" he said, patting Toby on the shoulder.

Kira shifted uncomfortably. "Mr. Bearclaw spent some time with Toby this afternoon, Rod," she said, "and they had such a good visit, he invited us to dinner. It was very kind of him."

"Yeah, real...civilized," he said with a wink. "I was wondering what the occasion was." Rod took another swig of beer. "Kira and I are close, you know."

"Yes," Bearclaw replied. "She speaks highly of you."

"I guess you'll be moving on pretty soon."

"I've nearly finished my business here."

"That's good, because I'm sure Kira's patience won't last forever."

"Rod..."

The businessman ignored her. "She's kind of soft-hearted," he went on, "so I hope you won't abuse her hospitality."

"Please, Rod, this isn't the place—"

"It's the truth, isn't it? It's what you said last night."

Kira was exasperated. He'd obviously had too much to drink, but that was no excuse. She scooted back her chair and got to her feet. "Could I speak with you in private?" she said.

Rod grinned. "Sure. Thought you'd never ask." He got up. "See you fellas around."

Bearclaw watched them walk out of the dining room. Then he looked at his son. "I don't care much for that man."

"Me, neither. And I don't like his bratty daughter, either. She's in my class in school."

"He's not very funny."

"Nope. I tell Mom that, but she doesn't believe me."

Bearclaw fingered his water glass. "You think she likes him?"

"Sort of, I guess. He likes her more, though. He was trying to kiss Mom last night. I could hear them in the front room."

He felt a twinge of jealousy, and it surprised him. Kira Lowell was an attractive woman. He liked her. He'd felt a strange rapport with her the entire day, a magnetic attraction that had been tempered only by the circumstances— their adversity over the boy.

The fact that she was white didn't bother him greatly, though he'd made a pact with himself to keep his romantic involvements restricted to Indian women. His last year of law school, he'd had an unpleasant experience that had soured him on cross-cultural relationships. For a year he'd dated an undergraduate, the attractive blond daughter of a prominent Denver businessman.

Ellen Macklin had professed to be madly in love with him, but when the day came to meet her family, she'd begged him to cut his hair and buy a preppy-looking suit. She'd wanted him to become the man she thought her parents would want for her. It was a rude awakening, one that opened his eyes to the realities. It struck him then that only an Indian woman could truly accept who he was.

"Mr. Bearclaw," Toby said tentatively, "can I ask you a question?"

"Of course, little brother. But if you're unsure what to call me, you can use my name, if you want. It's Joshua."

"Really?"

He put his hand on Toby's shoulder. "Sure."

"What I was wondering . . . Joshua . . . is if you ever saw my mother, my real Indian mother, I mean."

"I did several months ago. It was the first time in a long while. That's when I found out about you."

"It's really true, then, that you didn't know about me?"

"Not until then."

Toby grinned. "I guess I was a big surprise."

"Yes, a very big surprise."

"I know all about that stuff. Ladies' surprises, I mean." Bearclaw laughed. "You do?"

"Yeah. I got a picture of my Indian mother. I don't keep it out, because I don't want to hurt Mom's feelings. Anyway, I don't know her. Not like I know you."

"I'm glad we've had this chance to meet."

"Me, too."

"The only thing about it that worries me is your mother's feelings. She's afraid, I think."

"Afraid of what?"

"A new person in your life. It would be hard for any parent. But she has no reason to fear. I think you're close to her and love her very much."

"Yeah."

The waitress brought their salads, and Toby picked up his fork.

"What I was wondering," he said, "is if I could have a picture of you."

"If you'd like that, I'll send you one."

"Oh, boy! I'll keep it in my room. I don't think Mom would mind, since I kind of know you."

"Maybe you should ask her, though."

"Yeah, I guess I should."

Kira came back to the table. "Sorry, I apologize for what happened. Rod had too much to drink."

"He tells bad jokes, even if he's not drunk," Toby said.

Looking into Kira Lowell's lovely face, Bearclaw felt a deep fondness for her. "Out of the mouths of babes."

She nodded, then picked up her fork.

"What's that supposed to mean?" Toby asked.

"It means it's time to eat," she replied. Then she glanced up at Bearclaw, and their eyes met.

He took a bite of salad, contemplating the pact he'd made with himself after his misadventure in Denver. Kira Lowell, it seemed, had raised more questions than the ones obsessing him when he had come to Oregon to find his son.

Kira put her arm around Toby's shoulders as they stood on the porch, talking with Joshua Bearclaw. "You've had a big day, young man. I think it's time you head for bed."

"Do I have to?"

"Yes. It's late. Say goodbye."

He looked up. "Thank you for coming to see me, Joshua. And thank you for giving me the rug. I'll hang it up as soon as I can."

Bearclaw extended his hand, smiling. "My life is better for having a chance to get to know you, little brother."

Toby glanced at Kira as he shook his father's hand. "Thanks." He looked back and forth between them. "Are you going to leave Oregon?" he asked.

"Soon. I don't know just when."

"Will you come back?"

"Perhaps." His eyes met Kira's.

She felt her heart give a lurch.

"I hope so," Toby said.

"Off to bed, honey."

The boy started for the door. "Bye, Joshua."

"Goodbye, Toby."

When he was inside, Kira turned to Bearclaw with a sigh. "We still have some unresolved issues, don't we?"

"The future?"

"Yes. I don't know your plans."

Bearclaw looked up at the moon. "It's a nice evening, a bright one. Maybe we can walk for a few minutes."

There was a vaguely ominous ring to his voice, and Kira felt a touch of trepidation. "All right. Let me grab a sweater."

She went into the house and returned a few minutes later with a heavy cardigan. They descended the steps and walked slowly down the driveway.

The moonlight cast a silvery glow over the landscape.
Stars pierced the night sky. The air was fresh with only the
gentlest breeze. Though she wasn't really cold, Kira hugged
herself.

"You don't know what to do about Toby, do you?" she
said.

"No, I don't."

"Are you thinking of taking him from me?"

"No."

She studied his chiseled profile in the moonlight. "Can
I trust that?"

"I came with a simple purpose—getting to know the boy
and evaluating his circumstances—nothing more."

"Haven't you been able to do that?"

"Yes, but I find myself wanting more."

"Then you aren't satisfied."

"I would like to spend more time with him. But I know
it's not easy for you."

"To be honest, I'm more concerned about the future
than I am about now. I don't like feeling insecure...not
knowing what might happen next week, next month or
next year."

"You're afraid I'll use the tribal courts against you."

"It's better to be direct," she said, "than to beat around
the bush."

"We both care about Toby. I no less than you."

Kira stopped and Bearclaw did, too, facing her. "What
do I have to do?" she asked. "If it's his life here you're
concerned about, stay awhile. Do whatever you must to
satisfy yourself. There's a back-to-school night in a couple of days. Come to that with me. Talk to his teacher, go
see Dr. Olsen, the pediatrician, interview his friends' parents. Do whatever it takes." Her voice had grown emotional, and tears started to form in her eyes. "Just don't

leave me hanging." Her face crumpled. "I can't stand the thought that any day Toby might be taken away."

He took her by the arms and pulled her gently against him. Kira started crying. Her body was stiff, her fists clenched.

He stroked her head, comforting her. Her temple touched his cheek. She smelled the faint scent of him, felt the warmth of his body near hers. She pulled her face back and looked into the silvery shadow of his eyes. He was the man he'd been the night before, but now they were touching. His breath caressed her cheek, his fingers pressed into the flesh of her back. His solemn intensity penetrated her more forcefully than it had before. She trembled.

"Don't be afraid of me," he whispered. "I worry about my son, but I also worry about you. We are bound together, but there is more than that."

"What?" Her voice was a hush in the soft air.

His mouth moved slowly toward her, gently brushing against her lips. Her heart lifted as he kissed her deeply, the sweet taste of him permeating her mouth, his strong arms folding her tightly into the arch of his body.

She was swept away so quickly that she kissed him back, mindlessly letting her desire rush to meet his embrace. She kissed him hard, digging her fingers into his shoulders, running them up into the ebony locks of his hair.

"Kira . . ." he breathed into her neck.

And then her face lifted to the sky. She opened her eyes and saw the moon. A translucent cloud was moving across its face like a specter, and she saw the truth of what was taking place. He was kissing her, his tongue probing the shell of her ear, his breathing heavy with excitement.

"No, Joshua," she said, pushing him away. "No." She moved a half step back, incredulity filling her face.

He looked at her with eyes of a wolf. His expression was unyielding.

"That was a mistake." She sighed.

"If so, it was mine."

She backed up another step, forcing distance between them, fighting his allure. Then she shook her head. "Please leave us. Please go home and let us be."

He was silent, watching her motionlessly. Kira could take it no longer. She ran as fast as she could toward the house. When she got inside, she bolted the door against him. But it wasn't necessary. He hadn't followed.

After a minute, she heard the sound of his car starting. She tried to think of her son, of their life together, but all she could see was the look on Bearclaw's face just before he had kissed her. Then, with her head pressed against the door frame, she began to cry again.

Five

Kira was in no mood the next morning to hear Toby talking incessantly about his rug and his father. But she couldn't tell her son that, so she kept her silence, not knowing whether the previous night had been a disaster or simply a mistake. When the boy was ready for school, she drove him down to the highway to meet the bus, instead of letting him walk as usual, though she didn't know exactly what she was afraid of.

They sat waiting for the bus to come, and Kira considered warning Toby not to accept rides home—even from Bearclaw. But she realized there was no reason the man would kidnap her son when all he had to do was go to the tribal courts to get him. Her actions stemmed from her paranoia and her fear.

The bus finally came down the highway, stopping in front of the Jeep. She kissed Toby, then waved to the driver as the boy clambered aboard the bus. When they were out of sight, she drove back to the house.

Kira knew she would go crazy if she didn't do something, so she started cleaning, at first slowly and then, as she got going, with a vengeance. She vacuumed, then tackled the laundry and the kitchen. She was in the middle of scrubbing the sink when she heard the sound of a vehicle out front.

Drying her hands on a tea towel, she went to the front room and looked out the window. Joshua Bearclaw was getting out of his car. She cringed, feeling both apprehension and embarrassment.

Then she saw that he was carrying a bouquet of flowers. Obviously a peace offering. Relief passed over her, and she looked down at herself, realizing that she was dirty. Her hair was a mess; she looked terrible.

Bearclaw was on the porch. He hadn't seemed to notice her at the window, and Kira wondered if she dare not answer the door. When he knocked, she realized she couldn't do that to him, not after he had driven all that way. She opened the door.

He looked a little self-conscious, his eyes moving over her tentatively. "I've come to apologize," he said. "I lost sight of what was important last night. What I did was unfair." He handed her the bouquet of asters and chrysanthemums. "I hope you will forgive me."

He seemed so contrite she couldn't help feeling sorry for him. "You're not to blame, Joshua. It was my fault as much as yours." She smelled the flowers. "They're very pretty. You didn't have to do this."

"I wanted to."

She looked down at herself. "You caught me cleaning house. That's why I'm a mess."

"You look very nice, anyway. It's because you're so beautiful, and because I like you that I kissed you."

She laughed. "I didn't figure it was because you hated me."

"Am I forgiven, then?"

"If you'll forgive me," she replied.

They exchanged embarrassed smiles.

"Do you want to come in?"

"No, thanks. I took a lot of your time yesterday. I'll just go on back to the motel."

Strangely, she felt a rush of disappointment. "What are your plans?"

"I'm returning to Arizona, but first I would like to accompany you to Toby's school...see the place...meet the teachers and the parents."

Kira's heart soared at the mention of his leaving Oregon. He didn't sound angry, as though his intent was to bring Toby to the attention of the tribal court. It was important for things to end on a positive note. "Sure. You can go to the open house."

"I wouldn't be a bother?"

"Of course not." She contemplated a further gesture, afraid only that he might misinterpret her. But then she threw caution to the winds. "Would you like to have dinner with us beforehand?"

"I would be honored."

"We'll have to eat early, say five-thirty."

"That would be fine."

"Come at five then. You and Toby can play checkers while I cook."

"I look forward to it." He turned to go.

"Friday, at five," she called after him.

Kira stood at the door until his car disappeared over the edge of the butte, then sighed with relief. Sniffing her flowers, she went to the kitchen. It wasn't exactly a fresh start, but things seemed better than when the day had begun.

Toby and Kira were both looking forward to Friday. She'd told the boy his father wanted to see him again and visit the school before returning to Arizona.

Kira spent the morning reading the book on the Navaho she'd given Toby. Though her degree was in anthropology, and she'd had one class on Native Americans, she didn't consider herself knowledgeable on American Indian culture. Her contact with Bearclaw had sparked her interest. During the past few days, she'd even given thought to doing some course work on the subject once they'd sold the ranch and returned to California.

On Friday, Toby arrived home looking as though he'd run the mile from the highway. "Is he here yet?" he hollered, coming in the door.

"No, honey," she called from the kitchen. "Not for two hours."

"Shucks."

She peered at him through the door. "You've got chores to do and a bath to take before he gets here, so you'll be plenty busy."

"Oh, Mom. Can't I take a bath before I go to bed?"

"You want your father to think we live like pigs?"

"If you're clean, won't that be good enough?"

She pointed toward his room. "Go. Start by cleaning up your room."

Kira finished peeling the carrots and potatoes, and got the rack of lamb ready for the oven before going in to bathe. She was drying herself off when Toby pounded on the door.

"My turn."

"Awfully anxious, considering you hate baths, aren't you?"

"I want to get it over with."

She toweled her hair, deciding to dry it in her bedroom so Toby could use the bath. After slipping on her terry robe, she looked at her face in the mirror, remembering Bearclaw's kiss and his compliments about her beauty.

Kira had always been considered pretty. Her mother had taken her to a modeling agency in Portland as a child, and she had been offered a contract, but the time and travel commitment had been greater than they'd imagined, so they'd had to quit after a few jobs. She'd been homecoming queen in high school, and had been asked by a photographer in San Diego to model part-time while she was a college student, which she did on occasion, though she never really pursued it.

She had been a serious student with a deep interest in history and culture, though hardly a genius. And when Dan Lowell came into her life, she had no desire for anything else beyond a career in anthropology, and marriage.

As Kira applied moisturizer, she recalled her wedding at the church her parents attended in Seneca Falls. Dan wore his naval uniform, and six of his friends had flown up for the occasion. A picture of them exiting the church under the sword bridge had made the front page of the *Seneca Falls Beacon*. It was her mother's proudest day, and the happiest of Kira's life.

"Mom," Toby said, thumping the door with his fist, "are you still in there?"

"I didn't crawl out the window," she replied with a laugh.

"Now I know why Joshua didn't get married."

"What are you talking about?" She started gathering her brush and drier.

"I asked how come he didn't get married and have some kids, and he said because he didn't want to stand in line at the bathroom."

"He was teasing, honey," she said through the door.

"I don't think so."

Kira laughed. "All right, I'm coming out. But make your bath quick—I want back in to do my makeup. The light's better in here."

As she opened the door, Toby looked up at her. "Only reason I want in, is because you said I have to take a bath."

Kira smiled as she headed for her room. Glancing in Toby's door, she saw the Navaho rug Bearclaw had brought. They had hung it the day before, and Toby had spent hours lying on his bed, staring at it. She was pleased that he had taken to the man so readily, but it also surprised her. Toby tended to be shy, particularly around people he didn't know well.

She had wondered about that, trying to decide if it was because he needed a man in his life, because the idea of a father appealed to him or because of Joshua Bearclaw's personal magnetism. She suspected it was a little of each, but she knew the last factor definitely couldn't be discounted. It was what she attributed her own strong feelings to.

But the way they'd kissed couldn't be explained simply by the man's appeal. Kira was needy, vulnerable. There hadn't been anyone since Dan. Rod Banyon hardly counted, though she had to admit her loneliness and his interest in her had made her ask herself if she could possibly find a way to care for him.

Still, there was no rationalization of that kind with Joshua Bearclaw. She had every reason in the world not to form an attachment to him. He was an adversary, and he was from a different world. But he had been right about one thing—Toby did bind them in a way, though it was a relationship certain to generate frustration as much as good feeling.

What concerned her most was Bearclaw's appeal. She never recalled feeling so helplessly under anyone's spell. Even Dan, much as she loved him, never had that effect on her. She marveled at how easily she had succumbed to Joshua. One little kiss, and she had lost control.

Kira knew the slip couldn't be repeated. It had been unfortunate, but also a learning experience. Joshua might be special, and she might be needy, but he wasn't completely irresistible, and she wasn't totally without willpower. Especially when there was something important at stake—her son.

She dried her hair and returned to the bathroom to finish her makeup. Toby had managed to leave quite a mess. Using her "mother" voice, she summoned him back in to rinse the tub.

"When I grow up," he grumbled, "I'm going to have a house with a shower and no girls."

"I hope you're a very happy bachelor," she said, giving him a playful shove on his way out the door.

After she'd finished her makeup, she put on a long-sleeve green knit dress that was conservative, yet flattered her figure. Dan had always told her she had the best body in the world but, unlike some husbands, he didn't mind her showing it off a little.

There hadn't been many opportunities to dress up since she'd returned to the ranch. Jeans and a cotton blouse or a sweater had become her uniform. Dressing up, if only to go to Cattlemen's, had been the single most rewarding thing about her relationship with Rod Banyon.

As she glossed her lips, Kira wondered if Bearclaw liked sophisticated women, or if he preferred them homespun.

Had his experience gotten much beyond the reservation? And if so, what kind of women were they?

Kira knew what was happening. She had a crush on Joshua Bearclaw. He was good-looking, unusual and, fortunately, he would soon be heading back to Arizona. She might never see him again, though she suspected, because of Toby, he would remain at the fringe of their lives.

She went to the kitchen, noticing with amusement that Toby was setting up the checkerboard on the coffee table in the front room. Perhaps her son's joy at meeting his natural father was the bonus in all this.

It was quarter to five when Kira took the lamb out of the refrigerator. She would wait until after Bearclaw had been there awhile before starting to roast it. She put the vegetables on to parboil, then went into the living room and looked out the window. There was no sign of the vehicle. In the back of her mind she felt a nagging apprehension, as though there were danger.

She returned to the kitchen, and it wasn't long before Toby's shouts told her Bearclaw had arrived. Putting her apron aside, she went to the front door, which was standing open. The man was walking toward the house, Toby bounding along at his side.

Bearclaw wore black trousers, a white shirt open at the neck and a black vest. He made a rather dashing romantic figure, and Kira felt her heartbeat quicken at the sight of him. He was carrying a bottle of wine and wore an amused smile on his lips. He mounted the steps, chatting with Toby, then stopped in his tracks when he saw her.

For a moment he didn't say anything, but the admiration on his face told her a great deal about what he was thinking. Kira blushed. Bearclaw turned to the boy. "Did you know you have a beautiful mother, little brother?"

Toby looked at her. "Yeah, I guess, for a girl."

She laughed. "We're being macho today. Sissies are definitely out."

Bearclaw handed her the wine, then stood motionless, his eyes moving appreciatively over her features one by one. "I'm not a drinking man, but the fellow in the store said this was good."

She looked at the bottle, a California cabernet. "That was very thoughtful. Thank you." She gestured for him to enter.

He took a deep breath, seeming to inhale her as he moved past her into the front room. Toby was already on his knees in front of the checkerboard.

"Come on Joshua," the boy said. "Dinner's not ready, so we can play."

The man glanced at her regretfully as he went to the couch. Kira returned to her cooking, but her awareness remained with Bearclaw. His effect on her was remarkable, making her wonder if her loneliness had been greater than she realized. Or was he?

She put the lamb in the oven along with the vegetables. The salad was ready, but it needed to be tossed. She decided it wouldn't hurt to let the wine breathe. She got the corkscrew out of the drawer and went to the kitchen door.

"When Toby needs thinking time for a move, could I impose on you to open this?"

He looked up from the board, his eyes taking her in. "Sure."

"The bottle and the corkscrew will be on the counter."

After a few minutes, Bearclaw came into the kitchen. He removed the foil covering the top of the bottle, and they exchanged smiles. Kira picked up a towel and wiped some water off the tile next to the sink.

"Hope lamb's okay."

"I grew up on it."

"I thought you probably had." She watched him slowly turning the screw into the cork. "Looking forward to going back to school?"

Bearclaw let his eyes trail down her unabashedly. "Yes, but I've been looking forward to dinner even more."

There was something about the way he looked at her that was arousing. He wasn't leering, nor was he obviously flirting. It was a nonverbal statement of admiration, an anomaly she hadn't encountered before—a silent warrior.

"Toby's been excited for two days. You've made quite an impression on him."

"I believe there's a genetic thing between a father and son. It can attract them to each other or repel them. Sometimes both. The Indians would say it's in the blood." He set the lever on the mouth of the wine bottle and pried the cork from the neck.

"What about a mother and son...when there's no blood relationship?" she asked.

"There are many good feelings between people that do not involve blood, such as friendship, or the love between a man and a woman." He put the bottle down, then leaned against the counter, folding his arms over his chest. He stared at her with such intensity that Kira felt herself growing weak.

"Why do you look at me that way, Joshua?"

"I'm trying to understand my feelings for you—apart from attraction."

"You haven't lost your direct way of speaking, have you?"

He shrugged. "It's in the blood."

"Hey, Joshua," Toby called from the front room, "you can talk to her later. It's your move."

Bearclaw laughed. "You see what I mean?" He left the kitchen.

Kira's hands trembled. If this was a crush, it was the damnedest one she'd had since adolescence. Even Dan hadn't affected her this way. What was wrong with her?

She managed to get the dinner together and on the dining room table. Kira insisted that Bearclaw pour the wine, because she was sure she would spill it. They sat at opposite ends of her mother's antique mahogany table, the flowers he had brought the other day arranged in a low vase between them. Toby was seated to one side.

There wasn't much conversation during the meal, though their eyes met continuously. Kira made several remarks, but neither Bearclaw nor Toby followed on. She was nervous, acutely aware of the sounds of the flatware on the china.

Bearclaw only took a quarter of a glass of wine, but he refilled her glass twice. As he leaned over her, Kira was aware of his tangy cologne mixed with the scent of his own natural musk. She hardly moved when he was near, afraid—hoping—they might touch.

She only managed to eat a polite amount, having no appetite whatsoever. It was getting late, and they had quite a way to drive into town, so she asked Toby to help clear away the plates so dessert could be served. He brought in the last dish to her at the sink.

"Hey, Mom," the boy whispered.

She turned off the water. "What?"

"Do you and Joshua like each other?"

She blinked. "Why yes, I think so. Why do you ask?"

"The way you keep looking at each other. It's spooky."

She laughed weakly. "There was nothing spooky about it. When people eat together, they look at each other."

"Is that all?"

"Toby Lowell," she said, putting her hands on her hips, "are you jealous?"

"Shh!" he said, looking toward the door.

"Joshua and I are friends, fortunately," she whispered. "It's a lot better than if we hated each other."

He looked at her skeptically, but didn't say more. He returned to the dining room. As she prepared the dessert, she wondered if the chemistry between her and Bearclaw was so obvious even a child was able to pick up on it.

That was a danger sign. It meant things were getting out of hand, that an already complicated and sensitive situation was being further complicated by sexual attraction. Come on, Kira, she admonished herself, keep this thing in perspective.

But when she went into the dining room with the dessert, the patter ceased, and those marvelous eyes were waiting.

Six

On their way into Seneca Falls, Kira dropped Toby off at the Broyleses' ranch. Ed and Louise had been her parents' best friends. They had taken on the grandparent role, baby-sitting and taking Toby on excursions.

While Kira and the boy went inside, Bearclaw waited in the car. As she came out of the house, she felt him staring at her. Back on the highway, they rode in silence. She tried to relax, but she was tense. Bearclaw seemed completely at peace.

"Why is it I'm nervous around you?" she blurted out.

"Nervous?"

"Yes. Is it you, or the circumstances?"

"I've never had complaints before. You must be worried about Toby."

"That's probably it." But she knew it wasn't. It had nothing to do with her son.

"If it will make you feel better, you may as well know I'll be leaving in the morning," he said evenly. "Your life can get back to normal."

She wondered if he really meant it—if the danger was truly over. Still, Kira didn't want to press the issue. She'd let him leave quietly.

"I must be honest with you, though . . ." he said, pausing to find the right words.

Her heart picked up.

"It won't be easy for me. I won't be able to forget my son. Not now."

"What does that mean?"

He glanced at her. "That I would like to see him again."

A sinking feeling came over her. It was as though he'd taken off a mask. She was silent.

"Don't take that as something ominous. I'm not sure what it means yet myself."

"Then how could you know it isn't ominous?"

"Because I don't want you hurt any more than I want to hurt Toby."

His response gave her some degree of comfort, but Kira still wasn't sure what to make of the situation. Joshua Bearclaw was one of the most confounding men she had ever met, and her feelings toward him reflected it.

They arrived at the school a bit late and found the lot filled. They parked the car down the street and walked back. Passing the office, Kira saw Mr. Heartly, the principal, a slender man in his fifties. She introduced him to Bearclaw.

"You son's a fine youngster," Heartly said. "A bright cheerful boy."

"I am glad to hear it. You feel he's well adjusted, then?"

"I would say so. There are no signs to the contrary."

Bearclaw glanced at Kira before asking his next question. "Do you have any other Indian children in the school, Mr. Heartly?"

"No. There aren't many minorities in Seneca Falls. There were two Asian girls a few years back, but they're already in college."

"I see."

"We'd better get to Toby's classroom," Kira said. "We're already late."

Bearclaw shook hands with the principal, and he and Kira went to the third-grade class. Miss Engstrom, a plump little brunette in her late twenties, was speaking to parents who were squeezed into desks, sitting on chairs or standing around the periphery of the room.

Kira and Bearclaw moved along the wall inside the door, drawing the attention of a number of people. Kira couldn't help wondering if the others were more aware of Bearclaw's ethnic appearance or the fact that he was a stranger and in her company. As she looked around the room, she encountered Rod Banyon's sober gaze. He was leaning against the windowsill, his arms folded across his chest.

At Cattlemen's, she had been both firm and conciliatory, expressing her displeasure at his rude behavior but assuring him that Bearclaw's presence had only to do with Toby. Though his behavior had dashed any interest Kira had had in Rod, she saw no point in making an enemy. Judging by the look he was giving her, it hadn't worked.

Kira turned her attention to Miss Engstrom, who was reviewing the third-grade curriculum. Bearclaw was listening intently, his strong imposing countenance drawing the attention of the speaker.

Standing close to him, Kira could smell his cologne. She remembered his kiss, the flowers, the way he had been watching her. His remark about wanting to see Toby again paled beside their common concern for the boy. They were, after all, both parents of the same child, and they had a rapport bordering on romantic involvement. Strangely, the presence of other people made her feel protective of him.

When Mary Engstrom turned to write something on the board, Bearclaw whispered, "If this were 1880, Rod Banyon would be having me hanging from the end of a rope before morning."

Kira shot Rod a glance. "Why do you say that?"

"He hates seeing us together. I can smell it across the room."

"Rod has an immature side."

"And a hostile side, too," Bearclaw replied.

The teacher spoke for another ten minutes, then took questions from the group. Afterward, she invited the parents to examine the students' work.

"Come on," Kira said, "I'll introduce you to Mary."

She made the introductions and listened to them chat for several minutes. The teacher was polite and friendly, showing appreciation for Bearclaw's interest in his son. He questioned her about the way Native Americans were dealt with in the curriculum. When Kira felt a hand at her elbow, it was Rod Banyon.

"Could I talk to you?" he said.

She followed him out of the classroom. They strolled away from the building, onto the playground. Kira felt a sense of dread. She waited.

"Was it your idea or his to come here tonight?" Rod finally asked.

She started to inquire what business it was of his, but held her tongue. "I invited him."

"Why?" His voice was accusing.

"Because Toby's his son, and he wants to know about his life."

"Is that all?"

"What are you getting at, Rod?"

"I've got the feeling something's going on, Kira, and I don't like it."

"I'm not sure I see what right you have to—"

"I know we're not engaged, or anything like that," he cut in, "but it's no secret in this town that we've been seeing each other, and folks know I care for you."

"What are you trying to say? You're embarrassed that I'm being seen in the company of an Indian?"

"That's part of it. But—"

"I'm sorry if you're offended, but the fact of the matter is that I'm seen in the company of an Indian every day. If Toby's presence doesn't upset you, I don't see why Joshua's should."

"It's different, Kira, and you know it."

She turned to face him. "Look, Joshua's coming to Seneca Falls has nothing to do with me. He's here to see his son."

Rod took her by the arm. "Dammit, it's not just what you think I'm concerned about. It's him!"

A voice behind them made them both turn. "If I'm your problem, Mr. Banyon, why are you giving the lady a hard time?"

Bearclaw was standing ten feet from them, his arms hanging at his side, his face hawklike, intense in the faint light.

"I don't like people sneaking up on me when I'm having a private conversation," Rod shot back.

"I don't respect a man who abuses a woman over a problem he has with another man."

Rod drew himself up. "Now just a minute..."

"Joshua, Rod," Kira said, "this is getting out of hand. I don't want either of you behaving like a couple of schoolboys."

"I'm not taking insults from a redskin."

"There's no call for racial slurs, Mr. Banyon," Bearclaw said calmly. "I've expressed my reservations about your behavior. If you have any complaints, just say them to my face in plain English."

"All right, I will." Rod squared his shoulders. "I don't respect a man who uses a boy to impose himself on a woman's hospitality."

"He hasn't imposed," Kira protested.

"You may not see it, but I do," Rod said, dismissing her. "As a matter of fact, it's pretty damned obvious what he's trying to pull."

"Rod . . ." She glanced at Bearclaw, who was watching her, his face full of emotion.

"Look at him!" Rod said. "You think he's not after your body?"

"Please! Both of you," she cried. Several parents had gathered by the building, watching the commotion.

"You would know, Kira," Rod prodded. "Has he tried anything? Made any passes?"

She turned away in frustration, nearly in tears.

"Well?" he insisted.

"Dammit, Rod," she said, her back to him, "this is not helping matters. Joshua's leaving for Arizona tomorrow. He wanted to see Toby's school and meet the teacher. Why can't you just leave it at that?"

"You haven't answered my question."

She spun around, her face flushed with anger. Mr. Heartly was walking across the playground toward them. "This is juvenile," she said. "I'm embarrassed for all of us."

Rod studied her for a moment. Finally he shook his head with disgust. "So, that's the way it is." Then he pushed past Bearclaw, bumping his shoulder rudely as he went by.

"Mrs. Lowell," the school principal said, approaching them, "is there a problem?"

"No," she replied, "everything's fine."

He nodded, then turned back to the building.

"I'm sorry, Joshua," Kira apologized. "I'm very sorry that happened."

"It is my fault. I knew coming out here would provoke him. I let my concern for you get in the way of my better judgment."

She smiled weakly. Then, as they headed back toward the school building, Kira slipped her hand through Joshua Bearclaw's arm.

They walked for a while through the neighborhood. Kira still held his arm, though it was probably a more familiar thing to do than was warranted. But she felt an affection for him not unlike what one might feel toward an old friend, even though, underneath, his prickly attraction endured.

But Bearclaw was strangely quiet, contemplative.

"Why did you take my side against Banyon?" he abruptly asked.

"I didn't take your side. I didn't like the way he was treating you, that's all."

"That's rather shortsighted, isn't it? I'll be gone soon, and he'll still be around."

She turned to him. "Are you trying to tell me how I ought to behave? That's what Rod does!" She dropped her hand. "What is it about men that makes them feel they have to pull all the strings?"

"That is not what I was getting at. I was trying to understand you."

Kira stopped on the sidewalk. "What's to understand?"

"I don't like to be pitied."

"Is that what it is? Would you have felt better if you and Rod had fought it out like a couple of ten-year-olds? Did I deny you your masculinity, is that the problem?"

His eyes grew hard.

"Men!" Kira said, turning and walking up the sidewalk. She got to the corner and stopped under the shadows of a large tree. The streets were dappled with moonlight. She looked back. Bearclaw hadn't moved. She waited until she saw he wasn't coming, then she went back to him. They stared at each other for a long time.

"I'm sorry now that I came to Oregon," he said.

"Why?"

"You've made me uncertain about things. I'm not used to that." His eyes narrowed slightly. "I never thought I would care for a white woman again. I never thought I would doubt what I wanted."

Kira felt the muscles of her body tense.

He touched her cheek. "I'm not doing the things my mind tells me to do, Kira." His hand slid down her neck, and his fingers slipped under her hair at the nape.

She swallowed hard, having all she could do to keep from trembling. He stood an arm's length away as his thumb ran up and down the soft skin of her throat. She wanted him to take her into his arms, but he seemed to be holding her from him as much as he was holding on to her. His look and touch were hypnotizing, more intimate even than his kiss.

She didn't know what to think, much less what to say. It was maddening.

Finally, he dropped his hand. "I'm leaving tonight. I won't wait until morning." There was resoluteness in his voice.

They walked back to the car. Bearclaw opened the door, and she climbed in. He went around to the driver's side.

When he was sitting next to her, he said, "You're a good woman. My son is in good hands with you. Perhaps he'll grow up to be happy in your world. But in case he can't, he must know my world, too. I know that more certainly than ever."

As he started the engine, Kira felt her heart drumming. She didn't know whether to scream out in protest or wait till the storm cleared.

"If you don't mind," Bearclaw said, "I'll stop at my motel, pay the bill and get my things. It will save a trip back into town."

"Whatever you wish."

They went through the streets of Seneca Falls, but the familiar scenery passed in a blur. Kira's mind was turning. What had he told her? What was he saying?

He turned into the driveway of the Knight's Rest Motel, a modest place on the far side of town that catered to people preferring weekly rates. Kira wasn't surprised. He had only recently passed the bar and doubtless had no money to speak of. She thought of the dinner he'd bought them at the Cattlemen's, the wine he'd brought to the house, the airfare from Arizona, the rental car. She suddenly felt guilty.

Bearclaw drove to a cottage at the rear of the complex, screeching to a stop in the gravel. "I'll only be a few minutes," he said, pushing the door open.

He was passing in front of the car when a figure stepped out of the shadows. Kira's mouth dropped as she recognized Rod Banyon. When two more shadowy figures appeared, she knew trouble was imminent.

Without hesitating, she jumped out of the car. Rod's head whipped toward her. "What the—"

"She's with him," one of the others said.

"Well," Rod exclaimed, "what a surprise. I guess you're doing your whoring right out in the open."

"Leave her out of this, Banyon," Bearclaw said.

"You'd better worry about yourself, Sitting Bull," he replied, pointing an angry finger.

"Rod, stop it!" she screamed.

Bearclaw took a step toward him, and Banyon shoved him in the chest, sending him back several feet. Then Rod turned to Kira. "What happened? He trade you a night in the motel for the kid?"

She could tell he'd been drinking. The smell of alcohol wafted clear over to where she stood. "Rod, you're drunk and you don't know what you're doing."

Banyon laughed. "I know a whore when I see one."

He'd hardly gotten the words out of his mouth when Bearclaw was on him, taking him by the shoulders and throwing him over the hood of the car. "You watch the way you talk!" he roared.

The other two men grabbed Bearclaw from behind, jerking him back. But he knocked one away, catching him with an elbow in the solar plexus. Before he could deal with the second, Rod was back on his feet, grabbing him from behind. He had an arm around Bearclaw's throat as the other man punched him in the stomach.

Joshua grunted and Banyon spun him around, catching him on the side of the head with a roundhouse right. Kira ran forward as he fell to the ground. Rod pushed her back. She watched helplessly as the man Bearclaw had knocked down staggered forward and kicked him in the head.

"Come on," Rod said to his cohorts, "this idiot won't be causing any more trouble." He turned to face Kira, his body wavering. "He threw the first punch, remember that! We had to defend ourselves." Then he and the others staggered off.

Bearclaw was lying semiconscious on the ground. Kira helped him roll onto his back.

"Joshua, are you all right?" In the faint light, she could see that his cheek was cut. There was blood and dirt all over the side of his face.

He blinked, rolling his eyes a little before focusing on her. "God, law school really slowed me up." He felt his jaw. "There was a time when three drunks would have been a picnic for me."

She brushed his hair off his forehead. "Thank God. I was afraid they'd killed you."

Bearclaw tried to get up, but he had to rest a moment longer.

"I'm so sorry, Joshua. This is all my fault. This wouldn't have happened if it weren't for me."

"It might have been worse if you weren't here." He flexed his arm.

"Is anything broken? Are you badly hurt?"

He wiped the blood from the side of his face and looked at his hand in the moonlight. "I'll live." He managed to sit up. Then he got to his feet, leaning for a second against the front of the car.

"I'd better drive you to the hospital. You may need some stitches."

"No, I'll just go inside and wash myself off. If I can stop the bleeding, I'll tape the cut closed. The scar's smaller that way." He stood up and she took him by the arm.

As they reached the door of the cottage, Bearclaw fished the key from his pocket.

"You can wait in the car, if you like. You probably don't want to be seen going in here with me."

"The hell with Rod, or anyone else who cares," she replied. "He provoked that fight, and I'll tell anybody so who asks."

He got the door open and went inside. After he turned on a light, he stumbled toward the bathroom.

"Need some help?" she called after him.

"No, I used to be pretty good at this." Turning on the faucet, he leaned over the basin.

Kira closed the door and glanced around the room. It was modest, but very neat. Clothes were hanging in the curtained closet in one corner of the room; his things were arranged in an orderly fashion on the dresser and nightstand.

She glanced in the bathroom. He was splashing water on his face. After he examined himself in the mirror, he looked at her.

"I certainly hope you don't feel any shame. I'm totally disgusted with Rod. This was not only unnecessary, it was unfair."

"I should have been able to take them anyway, considering how drunk they were."

"Don't say that, Joshua," she said. "I would have had to feel sorry for them instead of you, if you'd knocked them out." She went to the bathroom door.

Up close she could see his swollen cheekbone and the puffiness that extended to the corner of his eye.

"You poor man," she said, feeling his pain.

He shrugged. "It was a lesson." He pointed to his other cheek. "Fortunately, they didn't get me on my good side."

Kira touched his battered flesh with the tip of her fingers. He turned his head to kiss her hand.

She remembered the way he'd touched her earlier, before Rod's sudden appearance. This time, rather than holding her away, he let her drift into his arms. As his mouth moved toward her, Kira parted her lips to accept his kiss.

They had barely embraced when they heard the sound of a vehicle outside. A car door slammed, and seconds later they heard a loud knocking. They both turned, and through the curtains saw flashing red and white lights.

"We've got company." Bearclaw walked to the door and pulled it open. A uniformed deputy sheriff was standing tall in the doorway, his thumbs tucked in his utility belt. There was another officer, a somewhat smaller man, behind him. "Your name Bearclaw?" the first officer said.

"Yes."

"A complaint's been made out against you for assault. We got to take you in."

"Assault?" Kira said, walking to the door.

The deputy looked past Bearclaw at her. "That's right, ma'am."

"Rod Banyon?"

"Yes, ma'am. Mr. Banyon and two other men." He gestured to Bearclaw. "Get anything you need. We're taking you to the county jail."

"This is ridiculous," Kira said. "*They* assaulted *him*. I saw the whole thing."

"We've got sworn complaints. If you're a witness, you might like to make a statement yourself, ma'am. We'll be glad to have you come down to the office."

"I certainly will."

"You have a J.P. in this town?" Bearclaw asked.

"If you mean a justice of the peace, sir, we do indeed. You'll be seeing him first thing Monday morning. I'm afraid, though, your weekend will be otherwise committed."

Kira put her hand on Bearclaw's shoulder. "Oh, Joshua."

He shrugged. "Now we'll see how the wheels of justice turn in Seneca Falls, Oregon."

Seven

Kira sat in a straight-back chair in the waiting room of the police station, watching the deputy methodically shift the paperwork on his desk. In the background she could hear the crackling of the radio in the dispatch room. Bearclaw had been with two other deputies since she'd arrived at the station in his car. She'd already given her statement and was beginning to grow impatient.

"They aren't really going to keep him in jail on the word of three drunks, are they?" she asked.

The sandy-haired officer shrugged. "He might be able to get out on O.R., if he's a lawyer like he says."

"What's that?"

"Own recognizance." The deputy grinned. "I guess whether he leaves or stays put for the weekend depends on what Justice Waitley says. Joe doesn't like middle of the night calls, though. Has a bad stomach. Doesn't sleep so good."

The door to the office opened, and the deputy who had come to the motel stuck his head out. "Type up an O.R. for Bearclaw, would you, Larry?"

"There's your answer," the man at the desk said to Kira. "Must be a lawyer, all right." He took a form from the desk drawer. "Sure doesn't look like one."

It wasn't long before Bearclaw came out of the office. He gave Kira a faint smile as he sat next to her. The side of his face had swollen considerably. He looked uncomfortable and in pain.

"How are you feeling?" she asked.

"I could use an aspirin."

The deputy glanced up from his typewriter. "Don't ask me for one. We can't dispense medication."

"I may have some in my purse," Kira said. She rummaged through it. "Yes, here's some." She handed Joshua the small metal container. "Can we have some water?" she asked the officer.

"Help yourself. There's a cooler around the corner in the dispatch room."

Kira brought the water to him in a small paper cup. When he had taken the aspirin, he looked at her thoughtfully. There was a touch of irony on his face, and sadness. It made her think about his struggle in the white man's world, the resentment she'd noticed in his letters, his concerns about his son's treatment by the community.

Except for Rod Banyon and his friends, Bearclaw's treatment in Seneca Falls did not seem to have been bad. There had been curious looks, but that was nothing to complain about. The people he'd met had been decent enough, even friendly. Yet, perhaps because of what she knew about his life, she felt a deep compassion for him.

The officer completed typing the document. Joshua looked it over, then signed it. The deputy who had come to the motel walked up to Bearclaw, his thumbs in his belt the same way they'd been before.

"Knight's Rest called to ask what to do with your stuff," he said. "I told 'em you weren't being held, but they said they already rented your room. Said you could get your gear at the office when you pay up."

"Oh, that's nice. Did they really rent the room, or are they trying to get rid of me?" he said sarcastically.

The deputy shrugged. "Don't know. You'd have to ask them." He handed Bearclaw a manila envelope containing his valuables. Joshua signed where the officer pointed.

"Any other places around here like that?"

"There's the Travel Lodge. Course, it's more expensive, and they don't cater to the weekly rate crowd. And there's places up and down the highway. I couldn't recommend any in particular. You'd have to check for vacancies. It's a Friday night, you know."

"Saturday morning, as Justice Waitley pointed out," Bearclaw said.

"Yeah. Saturday morning."

Kira stepped forward and took Bearclaw's arm. "Come on, Joshua, let's get out of here."

They left the building and went out into the cool night air. The empty streets were quiet. Kira led the way to the car.

"I'm awfully sorry about what's happened," she said.

"It's not your fault."

"It's terribly unfair."

"The worst part is, I've got to stick around."

"They aren't really going to pursue this thing, are they?"

"I haven't any idea. I'll know more Monday morning at nine, when I see the J.P."

They walked in silence. The news that he'd be staying suddenly turned everything upside down. Kira had been relieved knowing he was going back to Arizona, that their lives would be getting back to normal. Still, another part of her had been disappointed.

"Will it be terribly inconvenient if you have to stay awhile?" she asked, glancing up at him.

"I hadn't budgeted for it."

"If you're short of money, I can certainly loan you some."

They'd come to the car, and Bearclaw stopped at the door on the passenger side. He touched her cheek, as much in admiration as affection. "You have been kind to me, Kira, under the circumstances. And I've been nothing but trouble for you."

"Don't say that."

"It's true." He opened the door.

"I should drive," she said. "Your head must be killing you."

"I'm okay. Driving will keep my mind off my headache."

She got in the car, and he went around to the driver's side. "I'll turn the car in tomorrow. And I can exchange my airline ticket for one on the bus. That will buy me enough time to get things cleared up here."

He started the engine and drove toward the highway. Kira considered his plight. "Listen," she said, "why don't you get your things at the motel before you drive me home?"

"Why?"

She hesitated, having trouble saying what she'd already made up her mind to do. "Because I think you ought to stay at the ranch with us."

"That's crazy. I've already ruined your reputation in this town. You know what people would think if I stayed with you."

"I don't care about that, Joshua."

"You're not using your head. I'm going to be returning to Arizona. You live here."

"I don't plan on staying in Seneca Falls forever. Toby and I will leave as soon as the ranch sells. Maybe even before the end of the school year." She took a deep breath. "I wouldn't have said that before tonight, before you came along, but what's happened has opened my eyes."

"This isn't a bad town," he said. "Don't let what Rod and his friends did turn you against it. There are good people here, I can tell."

"Oh, I know that. It's not the people. It's me."

"What do you mean?"

"I've been...I don't know...kidding myself. I was never serious about Rod, but I let myself speculate on what it might be like marrying him, sharing his money and his small-town prestige. I've been sort of aimless the past year or so, but since you've come along, my eyes have been opened." She paused, looking out the window at the sleeping town.

"It's ironic," she went on, "when you consider that you're the biggest threat to my happiness. You're an enemy, as far as Toby's concerned. Yet, I feel a compassion for you. A certain identity. And . . . I like you."

Kira felt her eyes fill with tears, and it took her a moment to find the courage to look at him. He solemnly stared straight ahead, watching the road.

"You think I'm some kind of fool, don't you?" she said after a while.

"No. I already told you what I think of you. But I won't go to the ranch. I will pick up my things before I drive you home. Then, if I see a vacancy sign on the way, I can check in.''

They were at a crossroads. When she didn't object, he turned toward the Knight's Rest. Kira kept her silence, not knowing what to make of his response. She wasn't sure what she intended by the invitation, but she felt there was unfinished business. Maybe she had to stick her neck out and help a man in need.

When they arrived at the motel, Joshua went into the office to retrieve his bag. Minutes later he returned, slamming the car door angrily. ''They threw me out because of the fight. They don't need the room.''

Kira seethed. ''That's so unfair.''

He started the engine. ''These things happen when you're not a member of the Chamber of Commerce.'' He stepped on the gas, kicking up gravel as he exited the driveway.

They drove for a while along the highway, neither of them speaking, until Kira couldn't take the silence.

''Joshua, I insist you stay with us.''

''It would be unwise.''

''How so?''

''If you're too naive to look out for yourself, then I'll have to do it for you.''

''I'm not naive,'' she shot back. ''And I'm not planning to seduce you, if that's what you're thinking.''

Bearclaw said nothing.

''Sorry. That was unfair.''

He slowed at a motel, but the No Vacancy sign was lighted. He continued on.

''I still think you should come home with me. Earlier you said you wanted to see Toby again. That put a scare into me, just like when you told me about the tribal courts having jurisdiction over him. Maybe your leaving Oregon unsatisfied is worse than if you spend some time with him."

He glanced over at her. "I could end up spending a week or two here, depending on what Rod and the district attorney decide."

"We'll deal with whatever happens. Stay at least until your court appearance. Maybe when the judge hears what I have to say, he'll let you go."

"He won't take any testimony Monday. I may not even get to plead, depending on how they do things here. Chances are, he'll either set bail or extend O.R. But if they want to pursue this thing, I'll ask for a quick trial. In a little place like this, I should be able to get it within a week or so."

"You'll have to go to trial?"

"Who knows? My gut instinct is that if I want to end this thing any sooner, I'll have to find a way to make my peace with Rod Banyon."

"Oh, Lord."

They passed the last motel on the highway leaving Seneca Falls. Joshua didn't slow down, and Kira didn't even look to see if the No Vacancy sign was lighted.

It was too late to pick up Toby at the Broyleses' place. Kira decided she'd get him in the morning.

It wasn't until they'd turned off the highway and were on the gravel road leading to the house that the reality of what was happening struck her. She wasn't just a Good Samaritan, and he wasn't just a person who'd been badly treated. He was an attractive man who seemed as aware of her as she was of him. He knew she liked him, and she knew he liked her, though their conflict over Toby had muddied the significance of all that.

Joshua had been reluctant to come to the ranch. That either meant he was an honorable man or he was less naive about the dangers of them being together than she. But it was too late now to change her mind. He was going to spend the night in her home. The justice in that would simply have to prevail.

She glanced at him in the darkness, wishing he wasn't so quiet. His unexpressed thoughts began to concern her. She toyed with the idea of questioning him, but decided the best policy was to be matter-of-fact.

They arrived at the dark ranch house, and Joshua turned off the engine. He didn't move for a moment.

"Maybe I should sleep in the car."

He was giving her another chance, and his thoughtfulness touched her. But Kira didn't need another chance. Her sense of propriety was every bit as great as his nobility. She sat for a moment, trying to figure out how to tell him that.

"That time I let you kiss me, and I kissed you back, was an aberration," she explained, "if that's what's worrying you."

"I'm not worried," he replied without looking at her. "I just don't want to take advantage of you."

"You aren't planning on it, are you?"

"Of course not."

"Then what's the problem?"

"My leverage. I'm still Toby's father," he replied bluntly. "I don't like having a woman in that kind of position."

Suddenly, Kira realized what he was really saying. He wanted something to happen, but he couldn't use his advantage against her. That was the reason for his reluctance. "I see."

"Listen, it is not too late for me to leave."

For an instant she felt uncertain. But fearing what might happen was almost as bad as actually letting it happen. "This is childish, Joshua. We're both adults. You're here because you're Toby's father. You're my friend, and you're in need. I don't see any point in taking things further than that."

He opened the car door and climbed out. Kira got out, as well. While he retrieved his bag from the back seat, she opened the front door and turned on a light. Joshua came inside, carrying his case. In the light she could see how badly swollen his face was.

"I think you should have gone to the hospital."

"All I need is an ice pack and a couple more aspirin."

"I'll get them for you. Get yourself settled. The guest room is in the back, beyond Toby's room."

Kira prepared an ice pack and brought the aspirin and a glass of water to him. He'd taken off his boots and vest and was lying on the bed. It seemed strange seeing his long lanky frame sprawled out on the familiar furniture.

Propping himself up on an elbow, he took the aspirin, then lay back down. Kira gently pressed the ice pack against the side of his face. He was obviously in pain. She knew she'd done all she could, but she didn't want to leave him. The line separating compassion and attraction became blurred.

Joshua held his hand out, and she took it. His touch changed everything. Her awareness flared. She wanted to kiss him, to express the warm feelings she had for him, but she was afraid of what lay hidden under the surface of her emotion. She had to leave before it was too late.

"Good night, Joshua," she said, pulling away.

The corner of his mouth twitched. "Good night. And thank you."

```
*********************************************************
* You may have already won a lifetime of cash payments *
* totaling up to $1,000,000.00!  Play our Sweepstakes  *
* Game--Here's how it works...                         *
*********************************************************
```

Each of the first three tickets has a unique Sweepstakes number.
If your Sweepstakes numbers match any of the winning numbers
selected by our computer, you could win the amount shown under
the gold rub-off on that ticket.

Using an eraser, rub off the gold boxes on tickets #1-3 to
reveal how much each ticket could be worth if it is a winning
ticket. You must return the <u>entire</u> card to be eligible. (See
official rules in the back of this book for details.)

At the same time you play your tickets for big cash prizes,
Silhouette also invites you to participate in a special trial of
our Reader Service by accepting one or more FREE book(s) from
Silhouette Desire.® To request your free book(s), just rub off
the gold box on ticket #4 to reveal how many free book(s) you
will receive.

When you receive your free book(s), we hope you'll enjoy them
and want to see more. So unless we hear from you, every month
we'll send you 6 additional Silhouette Desire® novels. Each book
is yours to keep for only $2.24* each--26¢ less per book than
the cover price! There are <u>no</u> additional charges for shipping
and handling and of course, you may cancel Reader Service
privileges at any time by marking "cancel" on your shipping
statement or returning an unopened shipment of books to us at
our expense. Either way your shipments will stop. You'll
receive no more books; you'll have no further obligation.

PLus-you get a FREE MYSTERY GIFT!

If you return your game card with **all four gold boxes** rubbed
off, you will also receive a FREE Mystery Gift. It's your
immediate reward for sampling your free book(s), **and** it's yours
to keep no matter what you decide.

P.S.

Remember, the first set of one or more book(s) is FREE. So rub
off the gold box on ticket #4 and return the entire sheet of
tickets today!

*Terms and prices subject to change without notice.
 Sales taxes applicable in New York and Iowa.

"GIVE YOUR HEART TO SILHOUETTE" SWEEPSTAKES

DETACH HERE AND RETURN ENTIRE SHEET OF TICKETS NOW!

#1 $1,000,000.00

Rub off to reveal potential value if this is a winning ticket: ►

UNIQUE SWEEPSTAKES NUMBER: 6B 227073

#2 $1,000,000.00

Rub off to reveal potential value if this is a winning ticket: ►

UNIQUE SWEEPSTAKES NUMBER: 7B 229058

#3 $1,000,000.00

Rub off to reveal potential value if this is a winning ticket: ►

UNIQUE SWEEPSTAKES NUMBER: 8B 226724

#4 ONE OR MORE FREE BOOKS

HOW MANY FREE BOOKS?
Rub off to reveal number of free books you will receive ►

1672765559

Yes! Enter my sweepstakes numbers in the Sweepstakes and let me know if I've won a cash prize. If gold box on ticket #4 is rubbed off, I will also receive one or more Silhouette Desire® novels as a FREE tryout of the Reader Service, along with a FREE Mystery Gift as explained on the opposite page.   225 CIS JAYY

NAME

ADDRESS   APT.

CITY   STATE   ZIP CODE

Offer not valid to current Silhouette Desire® subscribers. All orders subject to approval.   PRINTED IN U.S.A.

DON'T FORGET...

... Return this card today with ticket #4 rubbed off, and receive 4 free books and a free mystery gift.

... You will receive books well before they're available in stores and at a discount off cover prices.

... No obligation to buy. You can cancel at any time by writing "cancel" on your statement or returning an unopened shipment to us at our cost.

If offer card is missing, write to: Silhouette Reader Service, 901 Fuhrmann Blvd., P.O. Box 1867, Buffalo, N.Y. 14269-1867

BUSINESS REPLY CARD

First Class   Permit No. 717   Buffalo, NY

Postage will be paid by addressee

Silhouette Reader Service ™

MILLION DOLLAR SWEEPSTAKES

901 Fuhrmann Blvd.
P.O. Box 1867
Buffalo, N.Y. 14240-9952

NO POSTAGE
NECESSARY
IF MAILED
IN THE
UNITED STATES

Kira went to her room. Quickly putting on her night-gown and robe, she went into the bathroom to wash her face. She could see a light under the door of the guest room and wondered if Joshua had fallen asleep without turning it off.

When she returned to her room, she locked the door. Kira knew she wasn't keeping him out; she was keeping herself in. Then she crawled into bed, utterly exhausted. It would be a while before she slept.

She pictured Joshua's pale eyes and battered face. She recalled his touch. As she stared into the darkness, she knew her feelings for him were special.

If she hadn't had the experience of a happy marriage, she'd have said she'd fallen for Joshua Bearclaw. But she couldn't afford to think that, not only because of Toby, but because there was no way she could have a relation-ship with a man who was so alien to her world. The irony was that he knew that, too, probably better than she. He understood that caring for her was impossible.

Lying motionless in her bed, Kira felt warm tears slide from the corners of her eyes into her hair. She was sad over the loss of something she never really had but something she now knew she wanted—a man named Joshua Bear-claw.

Eight

Kira slept late the next morning, and awoke still feeling exhausted. Even splashing water on her face didn't fully revive her. The door to the guest room was open when she left the bath, and she could see that the bed was made. But she wasn't going to check on Joshua—not until she'd dressed.

Pulling on her jeans, Kira realized that the Broyleses would be worried. Even though they'd said she should feel free to leave Toby until morning, it was already after ten, and she hadn't called.

The phone rang, and she hurried to answer it. Passing through the front room, she saw Joshua sitting in the easy chair, reading.

"Good morning," she said on her way to the kitchen, where she answered the phone. It was Louise Broyles.

"Glad to see you aren't wrapped around a telephone pole."

"Sorry, Louise. I got back late and just woke up. I'll be over to pick up Toby in a couple of minutes."

"That's why I was calling. Ed wanted to take Toby fishing up at Carson Lake, and I knew you wouldn't mind. Toby said you didn't have any plans for the weekend. Actually, they want to camp over so they can hit the water first thing tomorrow morning. I told Ed I'd call, and if it wasn't all right for them to stay over, I'd send word with Bob Cross. He's going to the lake this afternoon after he takes Elsa to the catalogue store."

Kira thought about how much Joshua Bearclaw wanted to see his son. And Toby would probably have wanted to see his father again, too. But she didn't know if she should have Ed drive all the way back that evening. "What time tomorrow do you think they'll be home?"

"By lunchtime. He said the best fishing's over by then, anyway."

"Okay. That'll work out fine."

She hung up and went to the front room. Bearclaw was wearing jeans and a fresh shirt. His cheek looked better. The cut was still taped, but most of the swelling was down. Kira felt a little guilty.

"Toby went fishing with Ed Broyles, and they won't be back until noon tomorrow. Hope that's all right."

Bearclaw nodded. "Sure. I can see him then."

"I could have insisted he come back tonight, but I thought..." She didn't know what she thought, unless it was that she preferred to spend the time with Joshua alone. Though she didn't know to what end.

He smiled, taking her in with that frank sweeping glance of his. "Don't worry about it."

Her awareness of him made a mockery of all the convictions she'd formed the night before. It didn't matter how impossible things were between them. She covered her confusion by asking if he was hungry.

"I could eat."

"Want to start with coffee?"

"Sounds good."

Kira went to the kitchen. Bearclaw followed her. He sat down at the table and watched while she put the coffee on. "Eggs? Pancakes?" she said, turning to him. "How hungry are you?"

"What do you normally have for breakfast?"

"Toast," she said, patting her hip. "I like pancakes, French toast and all that, but they don't like me. But I'll fix whatever you want."

"Toast is fine."

"Jam and an egg?"

"All right." He watched her in silence. "I'm not used to having a woman cook for me," he said after a while.

"You an inveterate bachelor?"

"I guess you could say that."

Kira was busy and didn't look at him. "How come you never married? Didn't you find anyone you wanted?"

"I found someone once, but it didn't work out."

She glanced back at him. "What happened?"

"She was white, I was an Indian. She didn't fully appreciate what that meant, but her father did."

"That explains your sensitivities."

"It explains my realism."

She stopped to look at him. "Are you bitter, Joshua?"

"I'd like to think I wasn't. The truth is I might be, a little. But Ellen's well in the past now, and my life's taken a different orientation."

Kira made the toast, poured them each a mug of coffee and served Bearclaw his egg. They sat opposite each other, the awareness that was always between them, building.

"You have any plans for today?" she asked.

"Not other than to stay out of your hair. How about you?"

"No. I guess I should have insisted Ed bring Toby back this afternoon. At least you wouldn't be bored."

There must have been more hurt in her voice than she realized, because Bearclaw was quick to justify himself. "I didn't mean to suggest you were boring," he said. "I just don't want to be in your way."

"You're free to do whatever you wish."

"Perhaps I'll hike back up the mountain. It looked like there was some pretty country up there when I walked over the hill with Toby."

"Dad used to like to ride up that way. I'd go with him sometimes, when I was a kid."

"Do you ride?"

"Not recently. I sold my dad's horses first thing. It took too much to keep them. On some days, though, I wish I had one to saddle up and ride into the mountains."

"Walking's not bad. Want to come with me?"

Kira was surprised at the invitation. By the look on Bearclaw's face, she judged it had been a spontaneous sort of thing, like when she'd invited him back to the ranch the night before. "You wouldn't mind?"

"I wouldn't have invited you if I did."

"I could fix a lunch. We could make it a picnic."

He grinned insouciantly.

"Are you sure you want me along?"

"There is enough room under the open sky that we won't step on each other's toes." His gaze settled on her, winnowing the deeper feelings she'd been hiding even from herself.

Bearclaw carried a heavy wool blanket and the lunch Kira had made in an old knapsack. He led the way through the wood and up the hillside behind the ranch house. Kira was breathing heavily by the time they reached the outcropping of rock where she had first seen him. They stopped for a moment and looked down on the valley.

"It's a nice view," he said nonchalantly.

"You were standing here when I first saw you on—when was it?—Monday. Lord, it seems like a month ago."

"A lot of emotion has flowed down the river since then."

"Things have been intense." She glanced at him. He was standing tall and motionless, in the same manner he had that first day. His expression was impassive. "You frightened me then," she confessed. "I didn't quite know what to make of you."

A slight smile touched his lips. "You did seem rather defensive."

"Wouldn't you have been?"

"In your shoes, I suppose so."

They stared out over the vista.

"How are you feeling now, Joshua?"

"Physically, spiritually or emotionally?"

"About Toby. About what's happened here."

He didn't look at her. "To be honest, I have mixed feelings. Nothing's changed, really. Except..."

She waited, but he didn't continue. "Except what?"

"The way I feel about you." He turned then, without looking at her. "Come on, we've got a lot of ground to cover."

They crossed the flank of the mountain, then climbed to a pine-covered ridge line, stopping again to look back at the valley. Kira sat down on a rock, exhausted. She was hot, though the air was pleasant.

Bearclaw had taken off the pack and was looking at the panorama of sky and distant mountains. He hadn't said anything more, and Kira wondered at his words. How *did* he feel about her?

She decided she must somehow be a problem for him. Perhaps he, too, was experiencing the attraction she felt. But could there be more? And if so, what?

"Rested enough?" he asked.

She looked up at him. "Joshua, are we in a hurry?"

He grinned. "I like to cover ground when I walk."

"You might have to do it with me on your back, if we go any faster. When are we going to eat, anyway?"

"Are you hungry?"

"No, but at least I'll be able to sit down for a while."

He laughed. "I hadn't planned on going much farther. There's undoubtedly a stream in the valley behind us. Maybe we can find a spot along it somewhere."

He gave her a few more minutes of rest, then pulled her to her feet. He smiled faintly before releasing her hand, then swung the pack onto his shoulder and headed down through the pine forest.

They came to the stream before long. Kira was thirsty and climbed down the bank so she could cup some water with her hand. Then she splashed some onto her face before running her fingers under her hair at the back of her neck. When she rose, she saw Bearclaw above her on the bank. He was watching her with an intense somber look in his eyes. She smiled, but his expression didn't change. She wanted to ask him what the matter was, but she knew. His feelings for her had changed.

"Had enough water?"

She nodded. He offered his hand again, then pulled her up the bank with great strength. The force of his effort brought their bodies together. There faces were close, but Bearclaw released her and moved back.

"Let's head upstream and see if we can find that water-fall I hear," he said before turning away.

Kira watched him go ahead of her, wondering why he hadn't kissed her. He could have, and though she hadn't intended that it happen, she would have let him. Perhaps he knew that and didn't like the idea. Maybe this change of feelings he spoke of was negative.

Bearclaw stopped to look back. Kira hadn't moved. "Coming?" he called to her.

"Yes, Joshua, I'm coming."

They moved upstream a hundred yards, finding the wa-terfall he had heard. It was an idyllic spot. Below the fall was a pool surrounded by ferns. On the bank above was a tiny glen with a fallen log on one side and a dense thicket of saplings on the other two sides. By spreading their blanket on the floor of the glen, they were able to sit in comfort and privacy.

"What a beautiful place," she said, lying down. She listened to the steady soothing rush of the water.

"You haven't been here before?" He was sitting on the log, unpacking the knapsack.

Kira stared up at the lacy boughs that filtered the pale blue sky. "Not to this exact spot, though I vaguely re-member the stream. Parts of this area Dad leased from the government as summer rangeland. I came this far with him a few times, but not often."

"Hungry yet?"

"How about you?"

He joined her on the blanket, leaning back and cross-ing his boots. "We can wait awhile, if you wish."

Kira rolled onto her side, propping her head up with her hand. She looked at Bearclaw, and he looked at her. "I can't decide what to make of you," she said.

"Oh?"

"I'm getting funny feelings, but I don't know if they're negative or positive."

"They're positive. The negative ones don't have to do with you directly."

"They have to do with Toby, though."

He assumed a thoughtful expression. "The whole situation, I guess."

"Funny, isn't it? We're friends and enemies both, aren't we?"

"Maybe."

His gaze swept over her, settling on her face. He hadn't looked at her much that morning, but he did now. Kira saw how sunlight highlighted his black hair. Just looking at his angular handsome face made her feel strange. She tried to focus on his mouth. It was wide, sometimes stern, sometimes bent at the corners into the suggestion of a smile. His eyes were spiritual. They destroyed her, incapacitated her. His shoulders strained under the taut fabric of his shirt, saying he was a physical man, yet his overall appearance was cerebral.

"What are you thinking?" he asked.

She blushed. "How good-looking you are."

His expression didn't change. "You're brave, aren't you?"

"For telling the truth?"

"For saying it when there are so many things between us."

"What is between us, Joshua? Toby?"

"Toby and other things."

"What other things?"

Her insistence must have amused him, because he smiled slightly. "You're white and I'm an Indian."

"Is race important to you?"

"My people matter to me. They're separate from your people. Cultures don't mix well. One always swallows the other. And little fish don't often eat the big ones."

"You aren't saying you're afraid of me."

He shook his head. "I'm afraid of my feelings for you."

"I felt that way at first. But not now. I don't know why."

"I've made it safe for you," he replied.

She suddenly realized it was true. If Joshua had been cynical and selfish, he could have used her. "Why have you made it safe?"

"Because you're the mother of my son."

The words were simple, direct—and honest. Kira sat up, hugging her knees to her chest. She felt helpless, lost.

The air was full of the sound of the waterfall. A spot of sun fell on her back, warming her. She felt the need to separate herself from him. Getting to her feet, she stepped over the log without so much as a glance at him and worked her way down the bank to the pool.

The water looked inviting, so she impulsively sat down on the mossy ground, pulled off her boots and socks, then stuck her feet in the pool. It felt icy at first, sending a shock tremor down her spine. After several moments the coolness of the water seemed refreshing.

She didn't think about Joshua Bearclaw or Toby or even Dan. She thought about her childhood, about the times she would get away to some quiet spot to be alone.

She didn't hear Joshua approach, but she sensed his presence an instant before he touched her. His fingers brushed her hair. When she looked up at him, he touched her cheek.

That haunting solemn look that moved her so deeply was on his face. She turned to rise but he took her by the arms, practically lifting her to her feet. He didn't release her; he didn't step back. His fingers pressed into her flesh so deeply they almost hurt.

He continued holding her close, but their bodies didn't touch. Their faces were near, but he didn't kiss her. She could sense him doing battle with himself.

"Joshua," she whispered. It was almost a plea.

He kissed her forcefully then. It was as though he knew all along that she wouldn't have the strength to resist him. She didn't think about anything but wanting him. He was the force, and she was the object. He the instrument, she the melody.

She moaned and his tongue probed deeper, his lips crushing and caressing hers.

She grasped his shoulders and pulled him hard against her breasts. He took her bottom in his hands and lifted the front of her against his pelvis, slowly raising and lowering her as they kissed. The friction warmed her, and she had a sudden yearning for him to take her.

"Oh, Joshua," she said, forcing her mouth away from his.

He buried his face in her neck, and she tilted her head back. When she opened her eyes, she saw the canopy of boughs screening the sky. A blue jay soared across the open space, and she felt joy.

"I want you, Kira," he murmured. "I want you so."

She told him with her eyes that she wanted him, too.

Joshua began unbuttoning her blouse. When he had finished, he unfastened the top of her jeans and pushed them down over her hips. Then he quickly removed the rest of her clothing. Her bra came off last, and when the cups fell away, he replaced them with his hands, lifting her breasts gently. Leaning over, he kissed each nipple with warm moist lips.

Her buds engorged, and she found herself on her toes, pressing herself against him. He kissed her again, more gently than before, his hands sliding over her shoulders and down the cool skin of her back and buttocks.

When the kiss ended, she curled herself into his arms. She craved his warmth. She wanted him to take her, so she unbuttoned his shirt, as he had hers. Coming to the heavy buckle of his belt, she had to struggle to loosen it. Before she unzipped his pants, he removed his boots and shirt. Then he kissed her again and held her naked breasts against his chest.

Kira's hunger was too strong to wait much longer. She pulled down his pants, permitting him to spring against her belly. They held each other for a long time, their lips touching. Then they lay down on the mossy carpet, side by side, clinging together under the cooling mist of the waterfall.

Joshua ran his fingers along the side of her face, lovingly caressing her skin. Her head rested on his arm, and she looked into his eyes. What was it she felt for this man? Could it be love? So soon? It was certainly different than anything she had known. It was physical attraction, but she felt an identity of spirit, too.

Since Dan, she had only known the innocent love of a child, and she wanted more in her life. A woman needed a man. She needed affection and fulfillment. And Joshua Bearclaw was so much man.

He kissed her lower lip with gentle affection. His hand trailed to her breast, and he brushed her nipple until it became turgid. Then he moved his palm down to her mound. His finger found her moist recesses, and he began to caress her lightly, all the while his lips nibbling at her neck and shoulders.

Gradually, she lost herself in her pleasure. She rolled onto her back and opened her legs to his tender caress. Her excitement quickly grew.

He moved on top of her then, and she parted her legs to accept the full length of him. He entered slowly, feeling wonderful to her after years of deprivation.

The sensation was almost too much. Unable to hold back, she began to rock against him, taking in more and more of him with each lift.

Joshua began to thrust, too, at first slowly, in concert with her movement, then the rhythm of his stroke increased. Within moments, his excitement had surpassed hers, and he was carrying her along.

When she sensed his fulfillment nearing, her control left her. His power began to overwhelm her. Kira cried out at the pain, the pleasure. Then it happened.

Rippling convulsions spilled from within, washing over her body. The sensation died slowly, gradually fading into the pleasant reality of their embrace. Joshua collapsed onto her, pressing her into the thin mossy carpet covering the ground.

Kira sighed. Her arm slipped off the bank and into the water. She gasped at the unexpected sensation, but let it stay, liking the feel of it. Her head was just inches from the edge of the bank, and the ends of her hair were trailing in the water.

Joshua looked into her eyes. When he noticed her hair floating in the pool, he smiled.

"There must be a Navaho expression that describes the beauty of what I see," he said. "But if there is, I don't know it."

Nine

Bearclaw stared at the naked woman asleep on the blanket. The sun was shining through a hole in the canopy overhead, warming their secluded little glen.

After they had returned from the pool, they had lain in each other's arms for a long time. Finally Kira had fallen asleep, and he contented himself watching the rise and fall of her chest, the deep serenity on her lovely face.

He continued his candid observation, fascinated by the richness of her mahogany hair in contrast with the pale cream of her skin. Her full breasts were nicely shaped. Her waist was small, accentuating the voluptuousness of her pleasantly rounded hips. She was a remarkably beautiful woman, as lovely as any he had ever seen.

And he had made love with her, pinioning her in the forest. The mere thought of being locked in her was enough to arouse him again. And yet, he felt sad. Lovely as it had been, Bearclaw knew it had been an act of desperation on both their parts.

He had tried to resist his attraction for her because he had decided to take the long view—knowing he might, for many years, have to deal with her. How would it be, knowing whenever he saw her, that they had been lovers? After an affair was over, people were seldom able to look at each other without feeling the onus of what they had lost.

Now it was too late. They had made love and would have to face those obstacles. Bearclaw knew he would have to find a way to cope, not only for their sakes, but for his son's, as well.

A cloud drifted past the sun, causing a shadow to move over Kira's body. He could see that she was getting chilly, so he pulled the flap of the blanket up over her. She smiled and her eyes momentarily fluttered open.

"Come keep me warm," she muttered, reaching for his hand.

Bearclaw moved closer and she snuggled against him, her skin feeling cooler to the touch than his. He gently pushed her hair away from her face, and wondered what—apart from raw physical attraction—had driven her so. Was she lonely? Or was there more than that?

She dozed for several more minutes as he listened to the sound of the waterfall and watched the birds darting through the trees overhead. They would have to talk about Toby as soon as possible. Waiting, before telling her of his plan, would only complicate things.

Kira stirred, shifting her body to find a more comfortable position. She was on her side against him, and he saw her eyes flutter again. Then she gently touched his injured cheek.

"How's the cut?" she whispered.

"It will heal fine, as long as I don't smile too much."

"Is that why you've looked so stern?"

"Have I?"

She nodded, touching his lip and chin inquisitively, like a child. And then their eyes met. She seemed to be looking for reassurance. "It's all right to do what we did, isn't it?"

"As long as you aren't unhappy, it is."

"You're a wonderful lover..."

"But what?" he said. "There's qualification in your voice."

"There are other things we have to think about. I wish there weren't, but there are."

He stared off through the trees. "You're talking about Toby."

"Yes, but that's not all."

"What then?"

"What I'm doing to myself. I took a chance. I'm not protected."

He flinched.

"It's not a dangerous time," she said, reassuring him. "And I'm very regular. But I shouldn't have done it."

"I should have been more careful, too. But why didn't you say anything?"

"I don't know. I've been taking chances lately, inviting you to stay with us, for example. After you kissed me the other day, I should have known this could happen. Maybe, deep down, it's what I wanted. I was thinking of the moment. I was letting my desires guide me."

Bearclaw was silent. He looked into her eyes. They were so trusting. He didn't have the heart to hurt her. It was imperative that they talk about Toby, but this wasn't the time. Not while she was still in his arms. "Maybe I'm as confused as you," he said evasively. He kissed her temple. She was like a wonderful fantasy come to life, and he wasn't in a position to take advantage of it. Kira Lowell represented danger—a danger he hadn't been able to resist.

By the time they got back to the ranch house, it was late afternoon. They had come down from the mountain in a close companionability, Bearclaw holding her hand. Not much was said, but Kira sensed a change was occurring. Something was happening to Joshua, something was building. The impact of their actions was yet to come.

But she wasn't ready to deal with it. She needed time alone to think. While Bearclaw was on the porch, shaking out the blanket, she went inside to run a bath. "Make yourself at home," she called before she closed the door. "There's plenty to eat and drink. I'm going to get cleaned up."

When she was stripped and in the tub, she thought about what had happened. Closing her eyes, she relived the exquisite minutes by the waterfall. She pictured his face as she had seen it through her lashes—the hard edges of his desire. She saw his teeth clenched with the yearning of release and felt the pummeling of his body against hers.

It had been so perfect. He was a remarkable lover—considerate, affectionate yet forceful. Still, she didn't understand what it all meant. After Dan's death, she had been sure she would never be able to make love with another man without feeling guilt or sadness or shame. Joshua Bearclaw had been the first, and her feelings after the fact were remarkable for their simplicity. What had happened simply seemed inevitable. This particular man, coming at this particular point in her life, had been destined to make love with her.

Kira sank into the water. She was sore from their love-making. Her body felt wasted, though in a delicious sort of way. In the middle of her reverie, there was a knock at the bathroom door.

"You can come in," she said. "It isn't locked."

He pushed the door open. "Still taking chances, I see," he said wryly.

"What could you do to me you haven't already done?"

He grinned, leaning with his forearm against the door frame. "I've decided to take my car back to Medford. I should be able to make it there before they close."

"Do you want me to pick you up afterward?"

"No, I will get back on my own. I've traveled all over the country without so much as bus fare in my pocket. Besides, I could use the time to think. I imagine you could, too."

There was an ominous ring in his voice, and Kira felt surprise, then fear. But she knew not to challenge him. "Will you be back for dinner?"

"Don't wait for me."

She heard the distance. "Holler if you need me," she said, trying to sound cheerful.

"Don't get waterlogged," he replied. Then he turned and left.

She heard the front door close. She heard the car door slam and the engine fire. As he drove away, a funny feeling came over her. It was as if he was never coming back.

The house suddenly seemed very quiet. She felt empty. Joshua hadn't just gone, he'd left her.

What did the afternoon mean? Was it . . . just sex? Had he gotten what he wanted? Or was it that he hadn't gotten what he wanted—yet? *Toby!* Toby was in the background. Toby was the unspoken, unaddressed problem that had brought Joshua into her home and her life.

The bath no longer was pleasant, so Kira got out and dried herself. As she washed her hair in the sink, her mind turned. She alternately felt hurt, angry, distraught. After she dressed, she looked in the guest room to see that Joshua's bag was still there. It seemed like pitiful evidence of his existence.

Passing Toby's door, she stopped. The Navaho rug hung on the wall, making a bold statement she had ignored until now. Staring at it, the consanguinity of father and son seemed to scream at her. They were both Navaho. That was the basic fact she had tried to forget.

The man who had made love to her so exquisitely was a threat, a danger. But how could she explain her love, the tenderness and affection? Surely those were real, too.

She paced anxiously, her mind running away with her. She had to get control of her emotions. All Joshua had done was go away to think.

Kira pictured them making love in the forest. But she also thought of her son—the boy she had raised from the time he was a baby, the boy who kept her husband's picture on his dresser, who bore his name. What was happening to her? Was she destined to lose everything? Would her child be taken from her?

She knew what was wrong. Now there were two things she wanted in her life—Toby and Joshua. It was possible she would lose both of them.

She made dinner, but hardly touched it. She had no appetite. The uncertainty was gnawing at her brain. As the hours dragged by, worry competed with fear. She imagined terrible things happening to Joshua—accidents, fights, police, ambulances. She wondered if he might have gone to a bar or even flown back to Arizona. That seemed unlikely, considering his legal problems. The authorities would go after him. Besides, she knew he wouldn't do anything to hurt Toby.

She went to the front room and opened the door, staring out at the blackness. A cool wind was blowing up the valley. Autumn would soon be over and her life would have moved on. She wanted Joshua to be a part of that life, but fear told her that was foolish.

Listening to the distant sounds of the highway, she could hear the passing trucks. Joshua was probably standing by a dark road somewhere, trying to hitch a ride. Shivering at the thought, she went inside.

It wasn't awfully late, but Kira craved bed, a respite, though she knew her problems would follow her. She left the front door unlocked so Bearclaw could get in without waking her.

The bed was cold, and she hugged herself under the covers, waiting for her body heat to warm her cocoon. Then she listened to the wind. Eventually fatigue caught up with her, and she began to drift off. The last thing she remembered was the sound of the wind outside and her recollection of Joshua slipping up behind her at the pool and touching her hair.

The flatbed truck piled high with bales of hay rolled to a stop opposite the arched gateway to the Adamson Ranch, kicking up a cloud of dust. Joshua Bearclaw climbed down from the cab. He saluted the driver and stepped back as the vehicle chugged up the dark highway, its feeble yellow headlights barely illuminating the pavement.

He crossed the road and entered the driveway leading to the bluff at the eastern edge of the valley. The wind tugged at his clothing. An occasional tumbleweed rolled past in the darkness.

It was after three in the morning. The moon had already set behind the mountain ridge, but the starlight was sufficient that he could see his way. He didn't mind the darkness. As a boy he often ventured into the desert at night. Sometimes he would run for miles along the dirt roads, crisscrossing the reservation. Occasionally he would climb to the top of a butte to watch the sun rise over New Mexico.

Going home after a nocturnal foray was always the part he least enjoyed. But it was different returning to Kira Lowell. He had wanted to get away from her earlier because he had needed time to think. Once he'd dropped off the car, he had only one desire—to get back to her as soon as he could.

The long hours he'd stood at the edge of Medford, trying to thumb a ride, had been excruciating. Every passing motorist seemed to be conspiring to keep him from her. And when the cold wind had come up, he could only think about her warm bed and the fact that he could have shared it with her.

That afternoon, though, his mind had been in a different place. He had analyzed the situation. He had seen their lovemaking as a mistake, and he had resolved not to repeat it. But each minute, each hour that he was away from her, returning became a more important priority. Those futile hours he had spent trying to hitch a ride convinced him how imperative it was to be with her—at any cost.

He moved quickly. He had crossed the valley bottom and was approaching the bluff. Climbing it, he wondered what Kira's state of mind would be. Perhaps the time alone had worked for her the opposite way it had for him. She might have thought better of their relationship, decided it was a mistake. Cresting the bluff, he knew he would find out soon enough.

The silhouette of the ranch house was barely visible. His heart picked up in anticipation. His return had been arduous, but he didn't really know what he would do once he saw her. He figured she wouldn't be awake.

Silently, he climbed the steps to the porch as the wind whistled around the eaves. Before knocking, he tried the door. It was unlocked. Did that mean she didn't want to be disturbed?

Without making a sound, Bearclaw walked through the front room and down the hall. Her bedroom door was ajar, so he gently pushed it open. He could barely see the bed. Creeping near, he was able to make out her face against the pillow. She was sleeping; her expression was tranquil. He felt a rush of desire to hold her in his arms.

Carefully, he removed his jacket and boots, then unbuckled his belt and pulled off his jeans. After taking off his shirt and briefs, he lifted the covers and slipped in beside her.

Kira moaned softly as he eased against her. She wore a nightgown, but the skirt had bunched at her waist and her legs were bare. All at once she stiffened, lifting her head from the pillow. She pulled back to see him.

"Joshua?"

He laughed softly. "Who did you think it was?"

She rolled onto her back with a heavy sigh. "I wasn't sure you were coming back."

"For a while I was wondering if I would make it. There weren't many cars on the road."

"You should have let me come for you."

"It doesn't matter now. I'm home." He ran his fingers over her shoulder.

She grasped his hand, gently lifting it away. Then she held his fingers tentatively before letting go of them.

"What's the matter?"

She hesitated. "Why did you get in bed with me?"

He dropped heavily onto the pillow. "You are angry."

"I'm confused. I knew there was something wrong when you left. I don't understand what you're doing now."

He sighed.

"What *is* wrong?" she asked, turning her head.

"I left intending to figure out how to extricate us from this situation. But it didn't work."

"It's easy enough to solve, isn't it?" she replied coldly.

"No, it is not. I don't want to extricate myself." He lifted himself onto his elbow so he could see her face in the faint light. "Kira, I didn't even get to Medford before I realized I wanted you. The truth is, I can't resist you. I had to hold you in my arms, be with you, no matter what."

Despite the darkness, he could see the liquid of her eyes. Her mouth opened, but she didn't speak. He leaned over her then, their bodies touching as his face moved toward hers.

"Oh, Joshua..."

Her voice was pleading, but he wasn't sure if it was for him to kiss her, or not. It didn't matter, though. He would. He had to.

Their lips touched, and Kira lay very still. Her mouth was receptive, but she didn't move.

Touching her fired his loins. His skin was cold and her body felt warm and supple, inviting. He took her jaw in the palm of his hand, and her mouth opened wider. His tongue passed between her lips.

Kira moaned plaintively. It was almost a whimper. He cupped her breast, stroking her nipple through the fabric of her gown.

Joshua hardened, wanting her. He slid his hand past the bunched skirt of her gown until his fingers touched her fringe. His lips continued caressing hers. When his finger probed her, she encircled his neck and pulled him hard against her, kissing him feverishly.

Finally, her mouth broke free. "Damn you, Joshua Bearclaw," she said through her teeth. "Damn you all to hell."

He kissed her hard, feeling an urgent desire. Her pelvis lifted against him. He slid between her legs, and she opened herself, ready to accept him, ready to accept his love.

Ten

The sun was streaming in the window when Bearclaw awoke. He lifted his head to see Kira's face. A veil of rich auburn hair covered her cheek. Carefully, he brushed the strands away, revealing her lovely even features.

Seeing her sleeping next to him gave him a possessory feeling toward her. She was a woman he had conquered and won.

But *had* he won her? And what was his victory? His ancestors had taken women as part of the spoils of war. Victories were measured by different standards now. Emotions were more complex, the conflicts no longer primal, nor their resolution as simple, elemental.

Bearclaw wanted to kiss her. The woman possessed him, keeping his mind from the difficult issues he knew they would have to face. He felt weak beside his desire for her. Was it because she was forbidden? Because time would deny her to him?

He slipped from the bed, wanting to distance himself from his mounting anxiety. He wanted to do something for her. Serve her, as she had served him.

Bearclaw put on his pants and went into the kitchen. He managed to find what he needed to prepare her breakfast. When the tray was ready, he carried it to the bedroom.

She was still sleeping when he entered her room. She had rolled onto her side, facing away from him. The rounded curve of her hip showed under the sheet.

"Kira," he said softly, "I have something for you."

She barely groaned in response. Smiling, he put the tray on a chair and crawled onto the bed. He leaned over her, looking down at her beautiful sensuous face.

"Kira..."

She moaned again.

"I've made your breakfast," he whispered.

She didn't respond. He kissed the corner of her mouth, and her sweet scent made him yearn for her. He lay down behind her, letting his body cup her buttocks like a spoon. Still, she didn't move.

He plucked errant strands of her auburn hair from her shoulder, holding them between his fingers, examining them, delighting in their reddish-gold sheen.

Then, reaching under the covers, Bearclaw ran his hand up her thigh and over her hip, enjoying the velvety texture of her skin. Pressing his face close to her neck, he inhaled her again, savoring her distinctive delicate scent.

His loins strained at the rough fabric of his jeans. He didn't want to disturb her, yet he wanted her so badly.

Rolling onto his back, he unfastened his pants and slipped them off. Then he pressed himself against her naked legs. Kira moved against him, and he could tell she was now aware of his embrace.

"It's not breakfast you're hungry for, is it?" he whispered.

She groaned, lifting her derriere against him. The curve of her fit so neatly into the hollow of him that he wanted to press harder.

"Kira—" He hoped she wouldn't say she wanted breakfast.

She reached back with her slender hand and touched his face, stroking his cheek. "Make love with me," she whispered.

Kissing her bare shoulder, he slid his hand to her breast. She moaned as he gently massaged her. As her excitement rose, Kira pressed her backside more firmly against him. In response, he cupped her abdomen in his large palm, crushing her to him.

"Oh . . ." Her voice had the same urgency he felt himself.

He swept her hair off her neck and kissed her, dragging his tongue along her skin. She moaned again.

He probed her moist recesses, wanting her desperately. When she arched her back, inviting him, he rolled her onto her stomach, parted her legs and moved between them. Kneeling over her, he ran his palms up her thighs, over the rounded curve of each cheek and across the small of her back. He did it again and again, liking the feel of her flesh.

Kira's face was turned to the side. Her eyes were closed. His desire for her was too strong to wait. "I want you," he groaned. The sound came from deep within him.

"Take me," she whispered.

Bearclaw firmly grasped her hips, lifting her so that she was on her knees, though her shoulders and chest still rested on the bed.

When he entered her, she gasped, quivering under him. Then, as he began his rhythmic dance, she leaned into him. His excitement came rapidly.

She was at the edge, too. As he began building to climax, she called out his name, sending him beyond the limits of control.

She cried out as they reached their climaxes together.

Spent, Bearclaw collapsed, kissing her hair, her cheek, her shoulder. Lying under him, Kira purred with contentment, lulling him. When she reached back to caress his face, he kissed her fingertips.

Moments later, when they rolled onto their sides, their bodies still touching, he wrapped an arm around her and held her tightly against his chest. "Kira, Kira," he said with a sigh.

"What, Joshua?"

He groaned happily, feeling deeply fulfilled, content.

"What?" she asked again.

"I fixed you breakfast. Now the coffee's cold. I'll have to get you another cup."

"Don't leave me yet."

He didn't want to. It was so easy to stay, to hold her in his arms. He let his forehead touch hers.

A long moment passed. "This is crazy, what we're doing, isn't it?" she said, sensing that he was thinking about their situation. "We really have no right to do this."

"No right?"

"Toby will be home soon. Then reality will set in."

"Isn't this reality?"

She looked over her shoulder at him. "You don't mean that, Joshua. You know as well as I do how crazy this is— everything that's happened since we went up into the mountains yesterday."

"This is as it should be," he replied stubbornly.

"It feels good, I grant you. It feels wonderful. But..."
She ached, knowing how easy it would be to let herself
believe in what they had shared, what might develop between them.

"But what?"

She felt his breath on the back of her neck. "Joshua..."

He kissed her behind the ear.

She eased herself away. He moaned with disappointment. She felt empty, bereft, but the anxiety building
within her was worse. She rolled onto her back, where she
could see him.

"Toby *will* be home shortly," she said, her face turned
toward him. "And we'll have to deal with that."

"That's true. But we have to face this, too." He touched
her cheek.

"You're so hard to resist. I think, deep inside, I knew
this would happen the moment I saw you."

"I didn't expect it," he replied, "but maybe I knew it
would, too."

"Why didn't you expect it?"

"Because of Toby. I had very singular intentions."

"That proves my point," she said. "If we had any sense,
we wouldn't be doing this. At least I wouldn't."

He squeezed her shoulder. "Don't say that."

"It's true. I don't mean to spoil what we've had, but we
have to face facts. And the reality is pretty plain. You came
to Oregon to—"

"No," he said, stopping her. "I know all that. We both
do. The world is as it is, and we are as we are. We must deal
with these things, it is true. But our being together is no
less a fact. Why destroy it?"

"It's not that I want to destroy it."

"Then I propose we enjoy what we have as long as we
have it. Toby will be home soon. Tomorrow I must go to

court, and sometime very soon I will return to Arizona, as
I promised. Until then, we are together. We have this, and
I don't see how it is wrong that we do as we feel."

"On the lips of any other man that would be self-
serving. Coming from you, I know it's sincere."

"I am a man, like any other."

"No, Joshua. Not like any other." She smiled wist-
fully. "That's the problem."

They looked into each other's eyes.

"What time is it?" she asked, reluctantly making the
spell end.

"Almost ten-thirty."

"I've got to hurry!"

Joshua scooted to the edge of the bed and picked up his
jeans. "I'll get you some hot coffee."

Kira watched him pull on his pants, admiring his lean
muscular body, his straight black hair, strong cheekbones
and jaw. He was a wonderful lover, a remarkable man. But
she didn't know if she was capable of doing as he asked.
She didn't know if she could be that strong.

She was cleaning the kitchen when Louise Broyles called
to say that Toby and Ed had gotten back from the lake.
Kira promised she would drive right over to pick him up.
Bearclaw had gone outside half an hour earlier. As Kira
left to get Toby, she saw Joshua on a ladder against the
front of the house.

"What on earth are you doing?"

"Getting the leaves out of the rain gutter. It should be
done before winter sets in, you know."

"You don't have to do that."

"I'm trying to make myself useful." He grinned at her.
"Being entertaining may wear thin after a while."

She smiled through her embarrassment. "You sense I'm hard to please? Is that it?"

"I am not sure if you become easily bored. Regard this as insurance."

She dismissed him with a wave, then headed for the barn, where she kept the Jeep. She felt his gaze follow her and was confident of his admiration. It pleased her, but she knew that wasn't enough. The physical pleasures of a man could be wonderful, but they were never in themselves sufficient. That was what concerned her most—the other things she might grow to expect, to long for.

Driving to the Broyleses', Kira thought about what she would tell Toby. It would be best to let him know what had happened at the motel, and why Bearclaw was staying with them. That way she could prepare him for seeing his father.

Toby was glad to see her and came bounding out of the house when she pulled up in front. He was dirty from his expedition but full of enthusiasm and excitement. He'd caught three fish—more than ever before.

When he heard that his father was still in town, he grew more excited. "Hey, that's neat, Mom! How long's he going to stay with us?"

"I don't know for sure. Maybe just a few days. Maybe a week or more."

"I hope it's for a week or more. But it'd be fine with me if he stayed forever." Toby scrunched up his nose. "Is there anything a lawyer can do on a ranch?"

Kira laughed. "Your grandfather used to say there's a lot they can do to mess it up."

"But Joshua's not that kind of lawyer, is he? He told me he's going to help our people . . . I mean, his people."

"Yes, that's the kind of man he is. He wants to help others."

"Can't he do it around here?"

"There aren't any Navaho in Oregon. The Indians who are here aren't your father's tribe."

Kira went into the house to thank the Broyleses for their kindness. When they had said their goodbyes, they headed for home. She explained the fight to Toby and could tell he was upset. Driving up the highway, she noticed that he was being very quiet.

"What's the matter, honey? You tired?"

"No."

"It doesn't upset you that Joshua's back, does it?"

"No. I'm glad. I just wish he would stay."

She could see that Toby didn't like the uncertainty any more than she did. He had become more fond of Bearclaw than she had realized. Kira wondered what Joshua's appeal was. Was it the fact that he was Toby's father, or did her son seek him as a role model, someone special he could relate to? What would happen when Bearclaw left? Would Toby be better or worse for the experience?

There was a whole lot of uncertainty surrounding Joshua's presence. Yet there was something about it that seemed right. He was Toby's father. And, for the moment, he was her lover.

"Mom," Toby said, "there's one thing I don't understand. If that fight wasn't Joshua's fault, how come they're going to have a trial?"

They had left the highway and were on the road leading to the ranch house. She looked over at him. "Because Rod Banyon isn't an honorable man."

"I could have told you he wasn't very nice a long time ago. He's stupid, just like his jokes."

"I certainly won't be defending Rod to you, but I don't think it's a good idea for you to be bitter toward him. Joshua will take care of matters, I'm sure."

"Too bad those other guys were there. Maybe Joshua would have beat Rod up, and he wouldn't bother you no more."

"It's 'anymore.' But I don't want to hear you talking that way, Toby. Fighting is no way for people to settle things. Joshua stopped all that years ago. And if Rod hadn't been drunk, there probably wouldn't have been a fight."

"Still—"

"There's no 'still' about it. Because of the mistakes that were made, everybody will have to go to court. It's unpleasant, but at least it's civilized."

"Will Joshua win?"

"I don't know, honey. If there's justice in this world, he will."

They climbed the bluff and came in sight of the ranch house. Bearclaw was raking the beds out front and turned to watch the Jeep approach. Kira had hardly stopped when Toby threw open the door and rushed to his father. The two were still embraced when she got out of the vehicle.

For a moment she watched them in their joy. Again, she realized that they shared something that didn't involve her. And yet, she couldn't help feeling happiness for her son's sake.

Kira was in the kitchen preparing lunch while Toby and Bearclaw worked outside. She could hear them laughing from time to time, though she couldn't imagine over what. It pleased her that they had developed such a close relationship. But it brought back something she hadn't recently thought much about—Bearclaw's remark that he wanted to see more of his son.

With everything that had happened, that fact had slipped through the cracks. What did he have in mind?

Toby spending a week or two on the reservation every . summer? She sighed, knowing it would be tough to separate the man who was in a sense her rival, from the man who was also her lover.

That evening Toby and Bearclaw played checkers while Kira sat across from them, reading her book. The atmosphere was warm and familial. It had been nice in the past when the three of them were together, but now that she and Joshua had been intimate, the mood was markedly different. The relationships on all three sides had been fleshed out.

Watching father and son, and remembering their lovemaking, Kira couldn't help thinking what it would be like if they were to become a family—if somehow she and Toby's father could work things out to be together. It was a wild fantasy, she knew. Nothing that had happened, nothing that had been said, suggested it could be. Joshua had given no indication of thinking in those terms. And truthfully, it didn't seem possible.

Bearclaw was devoted to his people, and clearly there was no place for her on the reservation. If they were united by a profound attraction—even love—they were nevertheless separated by cultural differences and lives that had been disparate. Joshua could abide her, but he was at odds with the world of the white man, her world.

She could tell Bearclaw knew that as well as she. He was willing to live for today, because he knew there could be no tomorrow. It was very simple and very obvious.

Toby suddenly gave a happy shriek. "Mom, I won! I beat him!"

She looked at each of them, not sure who was more pleased. "Congratulations! Is this your first victory?"

"The first of many," the boy announced.

Kira and Joshua laughed. "On that note maybe you'd better have your bath and head off to bed, young man," she said. "Tomorrow's a school day. The bus will be here bright and early."

"Oh Mom, you spoil all the fun."

"I want you to grow up healthy and with a good education."

"Your mother's right, little brother," Bearclaw said. "Good habits in a boy make a good man."

"Ah, gee." Toby hung his head. He got up, giving them both a woebegone look.

"Don't forget," Bearclaw said. "You don't represent just yourself. You represent your family and your people. And also your mother. She's very important. You want her to be proud of you."

Toby responded with a feeble smile. "All right."

"See you in the morning," Bearclaw called after him as the boy headed off for the bath.

When he had gone, Joshua looked at Kira. His eyes were happy. "He is a good boy."

"Thank you for what you said. Being supportive of what I try to do is helpful. I appreciate it."

"You're his mother."

"Are mothers important in the Navaho culture?"

"No, ironically, they're not. Neither parent is as revered as in your culture. Children are raised by the extended family. An aunt or a grandfather may be practically as important to a child as his own parents."

"Then why did you say that about me to Toby?"

He winked. "It's my concession to the white world."

Kira looked at him for several moments, wondering if it was time to bring up the issue that had been nagging at the back of her mind. Deciding there might be no better opportunity, she plunged ahead. "And what will my concession be to the Navaho culture, Joshua?"

He contemplated her thoughtfully. "That's nothing I'll dictate. It's something we must decide together."

"When?"

"Not now. I must think about it sometime before I go, and you must, too." He got to his feet then, extending his hand. "I feel like a walk in the night air. Will you come with me?"

In her mind she saw them strolling together, arm in arm, kissing in the moonlight. It wasn't the sort of thing a person did with her rival, but Joshua was her lover, too. And he was inescapable. She stood. They got their jackets from the closet and went out into cool night air.

They walked without speaking along a path following the rim of the bluff. Bearclaw seemed reflective. There was something on his mind that he hadn't yet decided to share.

"Joshua," she said, breaking the silence, "we've got to talk about what you have in mind for Toby. I can't go on trying to put it out of my mind, pretending there's nothing hanging over us."

He took her arm then, his fingers gripping her. "I'd like to see him regularly, Kira."

"What does that mean? How often?"

"It depends partly upon the circumstances. I'd like for him to come to the reservation. Not only to see me, but his people, as well."

A jolt went through her at his words, though she knew she shouldn't be surprised. His idea wasn't inconsistent with what had happened thus far, and yet she felt as though this was what everything during the past several days had been leading to. This was the ultimate truth.

"Are you adamant about it?" she asked, trying to maintain her calmness.

"I'm not demanding it, if that's what you mean. It's got to be with your willing concurrence."

She was somewhat reassured. "I assume we're talking about the summer. A week or so? Is that what you have in mind?"

"Whatever you'll allow."

He was being conciliatory, which pleased her. But it also was a source of frustration. It put the onus on her. How could she resist him? How could she deny her son? "You are a hard man, Joshua."

"Have I been unfair?"

"Yes. You've made yourself irresistible. Both to Toby and me."

He didn't respond.

"Was it intentional?"

"What's happened between us is perhaps harder for me than for you."

She looked up at the moon above the mountain. "How could that be?"

"Because my life was destined, decided. I knew what I wanted. I knew my place in the world. I belong in Arizona, on the reservation with my people, not in a place like this."

"So?"

He stopped and turned her to face him. "So, you are here, and Toby is here. I am a stranger among you, and yet I care more for you than any two individuals I know."

The words were pronounced very emotionally, and they made her take heart, though she couldn't say why. It was apparent already that he cared for her, but the magic of his eyes promised more. They promised love—an impossible love.

She stepped into his arms and laid her head against his shoulder. She wanted to squeeze him with all her might, but she contented herself with letting him hold her. "How can something so wonderful be so terrible at the same time, Joshua?"

He didn't answer. There was no answer to a question like that.

Eleven

Bearclaw was already up when Kira, still in her bathrobe, ambled into the kitchen the next morning. He was sitting at the table, drinking a cup of coffee.

She smiled at him. "You're already up and dressed. Why didn't you wake me up?"

"I peeked in your room. You were sleeping so peacefully, I didn't have the heart to disturb you."

"That didn't stop you yesterday," she said, trying to keep a straight face.

"A moment of weakness."

"I take it you've overcome that particular flaw."

He grinned. "Let's say it's in remission."

She sat across from him at the table. The swelling in his face was gone, and only the small piece of tape remained as evidence of his injury. His eyes, his look affected her the way they always did. She hardly bothered trying to resist him anymore.

He was dressed in dark trousers and a white shirt, his hair damp and combed back. The comparative formality of his clothing gave him an official air. He got up to get the coffeepot. "Can I pour you a cup?"

"Thank you."

Joshua carried the cup over and sat down. He contemplated her.

"So, today's the big day," she said.

"I wish it was. Unfortunately, it may not be until the trial—if it comes to that—before we can be sure what's going to happen."

"I feel so badly about this. To be honest, I think I'm responsible. Your problem with Rod was because of me."

"Kira, you can't help what he does. I just wish I could figure out a way to resolve things quickly, get the monkey off all our backs."

"There's no chance it will be settled today?"

Bearclaw shook his head. "Not unless they take it upon themselves to drop the charges. Technically, the court won't be doing much more than arraigning me—that's what's normally done at the time of arrest. But I'll speak with the justice, explain the situation, see what I can do."

"Can I help?"

"Thanks. You've been a tremendous help already. If this goes to trial, your statement will help even up the odds."

Kira thought how different this problem was from their others. They were bound together in so many ways. Yet they were damned by each connection, too. "What would you like for breakfast?" she asked.

"Whatever Toby's having is fine."

"Cereal?"

"Why not?"

Kira smiled. "Speaking of Toby, I think I'll see if he's ready." She got up and headed for the door. "There's a whole shelf of breakfast cereal," she said, pointing. "Pick your poison."

She returned a few minutes later with Toby in tow. The boy was chipper. While he and Bearclaw ate, Kira fixed his school lunch. Then she joined them for a second cup of coffee and a piece of toast.

"You'd better be hitting the trail, partner," she said, glancing at the clock.

Toby took a last gulp of juice, then ran off to brush his teeth and get his jacket. Kira rinsed the breakfast dishes. When she turned from the sink, Bearclaw was watching her with an appraising and affectionate look.

"I'll get dressed as soon as Toby's off," she said. "We should be on the road by eight-fifteen or so."

He nodded, still studying her.

"Is there anything else I can get you?" She was trying to sound like the considerate hostess, to be supportive and do whatever she could to reduce the tension.

"No."

Toby gave a shout that he was ready, and Bearclaw went with her to the front door. She handed the boy his lunch and leaned over to give him a kiss. Bearclaw shook Toby's hand and tousled his hair affectionately.

"Learn a lot today, little brother."

The boy took off at a run, shouting his goodbyes. Kira and Joshua stood on the porch until Toby disappeared over the edge of the bluff. When she turned to go inside, Joshua was blocking the doorway, leaning casually against the frame. He didn't move. Their eyes met.

"No matter what happens with this legal thing, or whatever occurs down the line with Toby, I want you to know my feelings for you are very special."

His sincerity moved her. "My feelings for you are special, too."

Kira sat outside the courtroom, waiting. Bearclaw had said it was enough if she was simply available. She didn't need to be with him. The arraignment was obviously an embarrassment to him, so she sat wondering what would happen, what fate had in mind.

Joshua had put on a suit coat before they left the ranch. It was badly wrinkled, so Kira had pressed it for him. When he slipped it on, he looked devastatingly handsome. She sensed the suit was something Bearclaw wore to meet the white man in his own arena, but he didn't look uncomfortable. In fact, there was a presence about him that seemed to announce he could handle himself as well as any man.

When they had parked, they walked to the courthouse, Bearclaw very erect, dignified. She could sense the pride burning in him. She assumed he did nothing to indicate any special familiarity between them out of respect. But it was consideration Kira didn't need. As they had walked up the steps, she took his arm, feeling pride at knowing the man and being his friend.

Now she leaned her head against the wall behind the bench, questioning both her mind and heart. How could it not mean something that he evoked such strong feelings in her?

"Kira, honey, there you are!"

Conrad Willoughby was crossing the hall to where she sat.

"I was wondering if I might find you here," he said. "I tried calling you at the ranch first thing, but got no answer."

"Joshua has a court appearance, and I came along."

"Yes, I heard about that." He sat next to her. "Listen, I've been researching this business about the jurisdiction of the Indian courts...."

She started to say she wasn't worried so much about that anymore, that she and Bearclaw had pretty well worked things out, but she decided it couldn't hurt to find out what he had learned.

"The boy's father could certainly cause trouble for you if he chose," Willoughby went on. "All he has to do is bring the matter to the attention of the tribe. Under the statute, it can assert jurisdiction over Toby."

"But if he doesn't act, there's nothing to worry about, right?"

"Well, technically the rights aren't his, they're the tribe's. They could act independently of him."

"Why would they do that?"

"That's not a legal question, it's more of a political one. The point is, the danger's there."

"What does that mean? That I'm going to have to live in fear of the Navahos deciding it's time to come after me?"

"You never know. But that's not all I have to report, Kira. The good news is that I've checked into some of the case histories. It seems the tribal courts generally have been pretty fair and reasonable on this issue. They haven't made it their business to take kids from their adoptive parents out of hand. Most decisions that have gone against the parents have involved newborn and newly adopted children. There's no guarantee, of course, but the fact that you've had Toby for a number of years would work in your favor."

"You mean, I might win if there was a hearing?"

"It's certainly possible. There would have to be an overwhelming argument against you, or patent unfairness, in my opinion."

Kira contemplated the news. "What if Joshua decided he wanted Toby?"

"That's a hard one. I didn't turn up a case like that. I really don't know what the court would do."

She nodded. "I see."

"Let me know if anything happens," Willoughby said. "You would get either a letter of inquiry or possibly an order to appear, if they decide to take action. I've familiarized myself with the issue enough that I could help you, if it comes to that, at least in the initial phase of any action."

"Thank you, Mr. Willoughby. I feel better knowing that."

The lawyer said goodbye and left, hurrying up the hall. Kira sat thinking. What had changed, really? Nothing, except that being summoned before the tribal court didn't necessarily mean disaster. Should it happen, and they were at all reasonable, they would leave Toby with her.

She wondered if Bearclaw was aware of that. He was a lawyer, a Navaho and the father of a child adopted outside the tribe, so it was only logical that he did. A sudden wave of doubt washed over her. What if he had known all along that he might ultimately be at her mercy? Could that have been a motivation for their relationship?

She hated to think in those terms, but for all she knew it could have been a factor. Still, she simply couldn't believe that his feelings weren't genuine.

She waited nervously until Bearclaw finally came out of the courtroom. He looked neither distressed nor particularly pleased.

"What happened?"

"The justice waived bail, so I'm still on O.R. He agreed to expedite the case. I'll plead day after tomorrow and go through the pretrial motions. The district attorney doesn't seem particularly happy with the idea of prosecuting it. He told me he'd try to get the case on the docket the beginning of next week, maybe Monday. All that's the good part."

"What's the bad part?"

"Apparently, Banyon seems determined to see the thing through. I sense he's got everybody in his pocket."

"You mean they're prejudiced against you?"

"No. I doubt there's any overt corruption. But he's a local boy—I'm not. I'm concerned about getting a fair jury."

"Joshua, I don't think the people of this community will ignore the facts. Most people here are fair-minded."

"Maybe. But there are some ambiguities. When there's doubt, people will go with the dog they know."

"I can't believe you'd be convicted. I'm not saying my testimony would get you off, because I'm not known like Rod is. But my family's been here a long time. My father was liked and respected."

Bearclaw looked up and down the corridor. "How will they feel about you and me?"

"That's nobody's business."

"True, but Rod might try to exploit it."

"Is that legal? Can he raise something like that?"

"There are ways to get it to the attention of a jury."

Kira sat staring, her anger rising.

"That's the part that's concerned me most," Bearclaw said, "dragging you and Toby into my problems. Even if I'm convicted, I don't expect any jail time. It would most likely be probation or a fine. The damage to you two could be much worse."

She took his hand. "We'll do what's right, Joshua. No matter what."

That afternoon Bearclaw started to work on the barn. It was not in bad shape, but it hadn't been cleaned for more than a year, and there were some minor repairs that had been left undone since the previous winter. He was standing at the door, wiping his hands on a rag, when he saw Toby walking along the driveway, headed for the house.

"Hey, little brother!" he called.

The boy stopped. He had been looking down at his feet, moving at a mopey gait, when he heard Bearclaw calling. He waved.

"How was school?"

"Okay," the boy called back. Then he turned and continued on toward the house.

Bearclaw watched him go, wondering what was wrong. Toby had been enthusiastic and happy ever since he'd returned from his fishing trip. What could have changed his mood?

After putting the tools away, he went into the house. Kira was sitting at the kitchen table, a file and documents spread out before her.

"Guess what?" she said happily. "The ranch broker called to say there might be an offer on the place. I haven't looked at the financial sheets for a while, and I thought I would refresh myself before I read any offers that might come in."

"That's wonderful."

"Well, it's happened before, and nothing came of it, so I'm not going to hold my breath."

"Still . . ." He sat down.

"If an offer does come in, will you look it over for me? Unofficially, of course. No sense having a lawyer under the roof and not taking advantage of it."

He grinned. "A more important contribution than cleaning the barn, I suppose."

"I wish you didn't feel you had to work around here."

Bearclaw shrugged. "It makes me feel better."

She touched his hand, smiling. Bearclaw let his eyes linger on her lips. She had a pretty mouth. It was wide, the lower lip slightly full, sensuous.

She was so beautiful, desirable, in a quiet comfortable way. How could he feel so at peace with a woman whose background was so different from his own?

"Why are you looking at me that way?" she asked.

"It gives me pleasure to look at you. You're very beautiful."

She actually seemed to blush. Bearclaw thought about that night, how he was looking forward to being with her. On their way out of town that morning they had gone to a drugstore. She hadn't gone in with him, but he could tell that she knew why he wanted to stop.

During the long drive to the ranch, she had taken his hand and squeezed it affectionately. He knew she had been thinking about the coming evening, as well.

"At least one of the men of the house is in a good mood," she said, scooting her chair back.

"Yes, what's wrong with Toby? He really seemed to be dragging home."

"I don't know. He stuck his head in to say he was back, then went to his room. No snack or anything. Do you think there's something wrong?"

He shrugged.

"Maybe I'll go in and see him for a moment."

As she walked by, Bearclaw gave her a playful pat on the behind. She laughed, then skipped out of the kitchen.

He leaned back, smiling, his hands clasped behind his head. He looked up at the mountain through the window, remembering the day they had climbed up there and found their own private spot to be alone and make love. Why couldn't they live up there like that? It would be so uncomplicated, so natural.

The thought, the intensity of his desire to be with her, surprised him. He had known Kira Lowell only a week, but here he was, thinking of her in long-range terms, fantasizing about things that were clearly impossible. The reason was obvious enough. They were greatly attracted to each other and bound by the common love of a child. It should be dismissed that easily, he told himself, though deep down, he doubted that it really could.

Kira returned a few minutes later. She sat down, sober faced, shaking her head. "I don't know what the trouble is. He seems a little depressed but denies anything is wrong. I asked if he was tired, and he said he was. So I told him to rest before dinner. That's what he's doing now."

"He doesn't get this way often?"

"No. He's always been a happy child. The only prolonged period of sadness was when Dan died. He was so young at the time, I think half of it was mirroring my feelings."

Bearclaw looked toward the door, wondering.

"Maybe the euphoria of seeing you is wearing off," she said, "and he's beginning to come to terms with the fact that you'll be leaving."

"Maybe," he replied, "but somehow I don't think so."

That evening Bearclaw coaxed Toby into a game of checkers. Kira watched them, concerned for her son. There was definitely something wrong. Toby went off to bed before he was asked, which was unusual. She went in to tuck him in, though she no longer did that as much as she had when he was smaller.

"Something happen at school today that's got you down?" she asked.

He shook his head, watching her with his large dark eyes.

"Joshua and I are worried about you."

He didn't reply. Kira studied his face, hoping to find a clue, though none was forthcoming. So she kissed him and rejoined Bearclaw in the front room, telling him she didn't know what the problem with Toby was.

They sat quietly on the couch together, listening to music. Eventually, they got to talking about other things. Kira asked about his career plans. He answered in detail, recounting the needs of his people and the opportunity he saw to do some good. His eyes shone and his voice became animated. Kira knew he had found his life's work.

It seemed the time to tell each other about their pasts, not just in general terms, but the things that had moved and formed them. Kira told Bearclaw about her parents, the kind of relationship she'd had with them. And when he asked her, she told him about her marriage, the life she had shared with Dan Lowell.

It had grown late without them realizing it. All evening she had been acutely aware of her desire. But every once in a while, a fleeting suspicion that Toby was behind his feelings for her tripped through her mind. Just as quickly she dismissed it. There was nothing that Joshua said or did that made her doubt. It was only circumstance, and that was hardly grounds on which to convict him.

Their conversation had been a good one, and she was glad they had had it. They both knew they would make love in the future, but the talk had been necessary. When it was time for bed, Bearclaw asked her if she would like to take a quick walk in the night air.

And so they went out under the waning moon, masked by wisps of high thin clouds. They stopped for a while and looked up at it.

"When I was a boy," he said, "I thought those clouds were shadows on the moon. They were never visible except crossing its face, and so I didn't understand. It was a great mystery."

She put her arm around his waist and squeezed him hard against her. "Do you miss Arizona? Are you anxious to get back?"

"I do like it there. But I'm not anxious to leave you."

"We only have a few more days together," she said, "but I'm not counting them. I'm at peace. I don't know why, but I am."

"That's good. It's the way it should be. We really only have this moment when all is said and done."

"Is that the philosophy of the Navaho?"

"It's something everybody knows, but few people live."

"Do you, Joshua?"

"I have more recently than ever before."

"How recently?"

"The past week, in particular."

She saw him smiling at her in the moonlight. His eyes shimmered as he leaned over and kissed her lips tenderly.

Twelve

The next morning Toby was in somewhat better spirits, though still not himself. After he headed off to meet the school bus, Bearclaw went to work on the barn.

Midmorning the broker came by with a preliminary offer from an Idaho rancher named Sorenson. Kira asked Bearclaw to sit in on the presentation. The broker, Al Kinney, pointed out that the offer was for 90 percent of the asking price, which was good considering the market, and that possession wouldn't be until after the first of the year.

Joshua read over the offer. Kinney didn't seem too pleased about Bearclaw's involvement, though he didn't argue with his assessment of the offer.

"It's straightforward enough," Joshua said, "but there are so many contingencies that it doesn't amount to much more than an invitation to negotiate."

"Mr. Sorenson wants to know a deal is possible before he spends a lot of time and energy on the property," Kinney replied.

Bearclaw shrugged. Kira had some more questions for the broker. Eventually, she decided to counteroffer. When the papers were signed, Al Kinney left. Kira and Bearclaw had a cup of tea together, sitting at the kitchen table, before he returned to the barn.

That afternoon Toby came home in much the same mood as the day before. Kira was concerned, but couldn't get anything out of him. She and Bearclaw talked about it, but couldn't come up with a reason for his change in behavior.

On Wednesday morning they drove Toby to school and afterward went over to the courthouse for the hearing. Bearclaw entered a not-guilty plea after his motion for dismissal was denied. The justice set a trial date for the end of the following week.

When Al Kinney came by with a counter to Kira's counteroffer, she decided to accept it. "Now the real work begins," the broker had warned her. "The various inspections and approvals to remove the contingencies will take weeks." He estimated the chances of the deal going through were about fifty-fifty.

After the negotiations were over, and they were alone again, Kira put her arms around Bearclaw. "I've been wanting to sell the place from the day Toby and I came up here. Now that it might happen, I feel funny. This was my parents' ranch, the home I grew up in."

"That's natural enough," he said, kissing her forehead.

"You know," she said, "having you around is getting to be a habit. I've started relying on you emotionally."

"You're saying that's not good."

She nodded, fiddling with the button on the front of his shirt. "It's all well and good to think only of the moment, but the future can't help but crowd in on you sometimes. You'll be leaving soon. If the ranch sells, Toby and I will be heading back to Southern California."

"Is it a problem, my being here?"

She searched his wonderful gray-white eyes. "Of course it's a problem. Unfortunately, one I wouldn't do without."

"I can leave, find a room someplace. You don't owe me room and board."

She shook her head, fighting back the emotion that rose suddenly. "No. You'll be going soon enough."

He kissed her long and tenderly. As their lips lingered, she felt her heart thumping against his chest and his breath washing over her.

"How much time do we have before Toby gets home?" he asked.

"Two hours. Something like that. Why?"

He gave her a crooked smile. "I thought I'd knock off work early and get cleaned up." He touched her lower lip with his fingertip. "Could I interest you in joining me in the tub?"

They bathed together, Kira sitting between his legs, leaning back against him as he lightly massaged her breasts. Joshua kissed her neck and ran his tongue along her skin and into the hollow of her ear.

He offered to shampoo her hair. When it was rinsed and they had climbed out of the tub, he toweled it, drying her from head to toe.

"Were you the one who asked if I wanted to send you to a motel?" she asked, kissing him.

He gave her a seductive look that sent tremors up her spine. Then he picked her up and carried her to the bed. As she lay there, immobile, he began kissing her body everywhere, up and down her torso, her shoulders, her arms, her fingertips. At first she lay stunned, her skin electric from his touch. Then her muscles untensed and she relaxed into the sensation, luxuriating in his every caress.

When he knelt between her legs and ran his tongue slowly up the inside of her thigh, she trembled. Her body was alive with expectation, and when he touched her, she couldn't help a gasp.

Joshua lightly caressed her with his tongue, building her excitement rapidly. Minutes later she cried out in release, her hands clutching his hair, her body rippling underneath him. Afterward she lay breathing heavily, her heart loping in her chest.

During the next few days their life developed into a pattern. They worked and made love by day. Apart from the coming trial and Bearclaw's departure, their only concern was Toby.

Whatever was troubling him seemed to abate. He interacted more, but not the way he had before. Deciding it would be good for all of them to get away over the weekend, they drove to Ashland, where they managed to get tickets to one of the last performances of the Oregon Shakespearean Festival. The play they saw was *The Merchant of Venice*.

It was the first live theater Toby had seen, and though he was intrigued by the action, the costumes and the emotional voices of the actors, he didn't understand what was going on. Kira had tried to give him a rough outline of the story in the hope he might follow it, but it didn't do a lot of good.

On the drive home he leaned forward between the front seats, watching the road with them. "How come everybody was mean to that funny guy with the beard?" he asked.

"You mean Shylock?" Kira said. "Remember, I told you he loaned that other man some money, and when he couldn't pay it back, Shylock decided to get his revenge for the way all the others had treated him."

"How come they didn't like him?"

"Well, he was Jewish, and in those days, in that town, people were prejudiced against a person just because they were Jewish."

"What's Jewish?"

"They're people who share a religion and culture—one that's distinctive, different. At that time they were often moneylenders, too, which didn't make them very popular."

"Is being Jewish like being Indian?"

Kira and Bearclaw looked at each other.

"What do you mean by that, little brother?" he asked.

"Are Indians like Jewish because they're different?"

"Being different is not bad. The world is made up of many different kinds of people. Sometimes a minority will suffer, but it does not mean they are bad or inferior. Why do you ask?"

Toby shrugged.

"Do you think Indians are treated badly, like Shylock in the play?" he continued.

"Maybe."

Kira and Bearclaw exchanged glances again.

"Has something happened to you that makes you feel that way?" he asked.

Toby shrugged once more.

"It might be good if you tell us about it, little brother. Both your mother and I care."

"Nothing happened," Toby replied.

Bearclaw turned to him. "Are you sure? You've seemed sad recently. I thought maybe something had happened at school."

Toby scooted back onto the seat. "I'm tired."

"You don't want to talk about it now?" Kira asked.

The boy shook his head. Bearclaw reached back and patted his arm. Then Toby lay down on the seat. They drove in silence.

Hours later, when they arrived back at the ranch, the child was asleep. Joshua carried him into the house, and Kira undressed him and tucked him in. Then they returned to the front room.

She looked at Joshua. "I'm going to pick up Toby tomorrow after school and have a talk with his teacher."

Bearclaw nodded grimly. "I think that would be a good idea."

Bearclaw didn't sleep well that night. There was something in Toby's eyes that had cut deep into his soul. He wondered if it could have anything to do with him. Perhaps it was a coincidence that a problem should turn up now, at this stage of Toby's life, but he suspected it wasn't. He suspected that the incident at the motel was somehow involved.

The next morning at breakfast the mood was tense. Toby hardly looked at him. Bearclaw could tell Kira was worried. She made idle chatter, said the things a mother says to a son, but there was a brittleness in her voice.

When she said goodbye, Kira hugged her son an extra long time. There was a sad expression on the boy's face. Bearclaw felt a lump in his throat.

"Be brave, little brother," he said as the child headed out the door. Toby nodded slightly.

They watched him until he disappeared over the edge of the bluff.

"I don't know what they've done to him, but it's something," she said.

"Yes, I think you're right."

The day passed slowly for them both. Bearclaw cleared brush from where it was encroaching on the yard. It was hard work, and though the air was cool, he took off his shirt and managed to work up a heavy sweat. Just before noon Kira brought him some ice water. He stood drinking it, leaning with one hand on the shovel, his chest gleaming in the sunlight.

"I called the University of Oregon library," she announced, "and asked them to send me some books on the Navaho."

"Oh? What's the occasion?"

"I decided I should know more about Toby's heritage, and yours. Besides, anthropology is my field. I've even thought about going back to school and doing some advanced work on Native American culture."

He smiled with satisfaction. "I'm glad to hear that."

She looked at his chest and shoulders, her eyes brilliant in the sunlight. "You're a Renaissance man, aren't you, Joshua?"

"If you mean I know how to clear brush, repair barns and read real-estate contracts, I guess the answer is yes."

"I was thinking about your other...talents, as well."

He caressed her cheek. "It's those other talents that have gotten me into trouble."

"How so?"

"If I did not have a weakness for beautiful ladies with auburn hair, I wouldn't be facing an assault charge, worrying about my son and getting blisters, instead of righting wrongs in Arizona."

She touched his lip. "I'm sorry about the things that have happened, but I'll always cherish this time we've had together."

"If I wasn't so sweaty, I'd take you into my arms right now."

"Go ahead. I'm going to change, anyway."

He held her then, smelling her hair, touching her soft flesh, tasting her cool lips. She put her arms around his waist and looked up at him.

"I'm worried about Toby."

"I know. So am I."

"I think we're going to get to the bottom of it today."

"You are probably right."

"Do you want to come into town with me?"

"Yes. Unless you don't want me to."

She looked at him thoughtfully. "I've been thinking about it. We both know it's something to do with Toby being Indian...."

"But what we aren't sure of is whether it involves me."

She nodded. "Perhaps it would be better if it's just the two of us—Toby and me."

He pondered her words. "If you think so. There's plenty for me to do here."

"If you don't mind, let's do it that way."

Bearclaw went inside with her and they had lunch. Afterward, he went out to finish his work while she changed. When she was ready to pick up Toby, she drove the Jeep to the point nearest where Joshua was working.

"Don't worry if you see smoke on the drive back," he called to her. "I'm going to burn brush."

She waved, then continued on toward the highway. Bearclaw watched her go, leaning on the shovel. He understood her decision to handle the problem alone. This was, after all, her territory, not his. And though she in no way intended it as a slight, it was nevertheless revealing. It pointed up the fact that he was an outsider.

Two hours later, Bearclaw was tending the dying fire. A thin column of smoke rose into the empty sky. From his vantage point he was able to see the highway and the occasional vehicle moving along the ribbon of asphalt that ran down the center of the valley.

He had been watching the road more diligently during the past half hour, knowing they would be returning soon. Then, when he saw a vehicle turn off the highway, he knew it was the Jeep.

Bearclaw felt anticipation at seeing Kira. They had been together incessantly for more than a week, they were lovers, and he had grown accustomed to being with her. He imagined a good marriage to be comfortable the same way he felt with her, though he knew it could never remain this idyllic for long.

The Jeep disappeared from sight as it mounted the grade. Then it reappeared at the top. Instead of stopping, as he had expected, Kira drove on to the house. Bearclaw watched them get out. He saw her escort Toby to the door, then come walking out to where he tended the fire.

He could tell by her slow gait and her lowered head that she was upset. When she got to him, he saw that she had been crying.

"What's the matter?"

"Toby got into a fight today. His face and arms are all scraped up."

"He's a boy. These things happen."

She shook her head. "No. It wasn't just a fight. It was over what's been bothering him. Apparently, the word got through to the kids that Toby's Indian father was arrested for getting into a fight. They've been teasing him about it all week. That's why he's been acting strange.''

"Rod Banyon.''

"Probably.''

"Why didn't Toby tell us?''

"I don't know. Pride, embarrassment, shame, fear. Who knows what motivates a child?''

Bearclaw felt his anger rise, his heart begin to pump adrenaline. "What happened today, specifically?''

"I spoke with Mr. Heartly and his teacher, Mary Engstrom. They hadn't realized what was going on until the fight. Some boys were taunting him, apparently teasing him about his Indian blood. I guess the fight business came up, and they got into it.''

He looked toward the house. "I want to talk to him.''

"All right. But please don't focus on the ethnic part of it, the feelings of persecution that are already there.'' She touched his arm. "I know you're a prideful man, Joshua. Something like this is hard for you to take. It must hurt, knowing he's your son. But they're just children. It's a transitory thing. In a week or two it will all be forgotten. There's never been any trouble before.''

"Not until I came along.''

"It's not your fault. If anyone's to blame, it's Rod. You know how I feel about that.''

"Still, Toby's suffering. I can't stand by and see that happen.''

She sighed woefully. "I'm sure he'll want to talk to you. He's very upset.''

Bearclaw looked at the fire. It was burning low, but it still had to be watched.

"You go on in,'' she said. "I'll keep an eye on this.''

Kira watched him head for the house. She knew Toby respected him, admired him. During the past days the child had become confused. It had all come out during the drive home. The man who had become important in Toby's life was at the same time the source of his humiliation and suffering. Since there was nothing wrong with his father, he concluded the way he'd been treated must be his own fault.

The sun was getting low in the sky, and the fire had burned down to ash and coals. The air cooled, and Kira sat on a nearby rock, close enough that she could feel the warmth of the fire. She watched the house, hoping that things were going well between her son and his father.

Finally, Bearclaw came out. He wore a stony expression, similar to the one he'd had the day they'd met. She'd had a shotgun in her hand then, fearing him. How long ago that seemed.

This time, her heart went out to him. He was suffering, just as Toby was. His eyes barely met hers, but she saw that they were sad. He picked up the rake and began scattering the coals. Then he took the shovel and covered them with dirt. When the fire was completely smothered, he picked up all the tools and looked at her.

"You're right about his feelings," he said. "We had a good talk. I tried to make it positive. I tried to reinforce his confidence and his pride. I didn't make it a matter of the white man versus the Indian."

"I'm sure you said the right thing."

"I have to go somewhere and think, Kira. There are many things on my mind. I'll put the tools away, and then I'll walk. I'll go up on the mountain."

She wanted to console him. She touched his arm. There was a glaze of emotion in his eyes, but his jaw was set. The resolution she had seen that first day returned. "Please don't hate, Joshua."

He didn't move. He seemed barely to breathe. She leaned forward and kissed his cheek. "I love you," she whispered.

His eyes seemed suddenly to flood, though he didn't flinch, he didn't stir. Then, slowly, his eyes cleared. "You are a good woman," he said in a low emotional voice. "I knew that the minute I saw you."

She tried to smile. "Even with Dad's shotgun in my hand?"

He dropped the tools, reached out and pulled her against his chest. His arms were locked around her. He kissed her hair, then cupped her jaw in his hands. "You are a good person," he whispered. "I'll never forget what you have done." Then he picked up the tools and headed off toward the barn.

Thirteen

As evening came, Kira sat at the kitchen table, looking up at the hill behind the house. For half an hour Bearclaw had been on the rocks where she had first seen him. He was sitting at the moment, motionless, staring out at the encroaching darkness.

She could imagine the things he was thinking. Life had given him yet another rude awakening after the brief taste of happiness they'd shared. They both had known their times together were temporary, but the fact that Toby had been hurt had to make Bearclaw bitter.

Kira was heartsick. She was upset because of what had happened to her son, but she felt even worse about what Joshua was going through. It was so undeserved. Worst of all, she could do nothing about it. It wasn't enough that she cared for him or that he cared for her. The problem was the circumstances: who Joshua was, what he believed in, what mattered in his life.

There was no doubt in Kira's mind that Joshua would always be a fighter, though he had gone beyond using his fists. But more than that, the incident with Toby had convinced her that she and Bearclaw lived on different planets. They had their friendship in common. They could live with each other, but not together in the world. She had known that even before she had fallen in love with him. She had never doubted it; she simply had decided to push it aside for a few days to be with him.

Her eyes glistened as she stared at the distant lonely figure. He was slipping away from her. Toby's problem had hit them both like a splash of cold water. Now it was time to come back down to earth.

Dan's death had been the greatest tragedy of her life. Death had to be accepted; there was no alternative. But seeing someone pulled slowly away, as if by an ineluctable current, and being able to look into their eyes and read the sadness as your fingers slipped apart from theirs—that was torture. Still, Kira had been willing to pay the price.

What would Bearclaw do? There was an unfathomable aspect to the man, an inner place she hadn't been able to penetrate. He was honorable, she knew that. But he was unpredictable, too.

Bearclaw was a loner, a latter-day warrior. Ultimately, he relied only on himself. He could love, he could sacrifice, but in the end he went to the mountain alone. It was a story from a different age, values that ignored the era, beliefs that paid no heed to time.

Yet she loved him. Kira could truly say that, though she didn't know him, not as she had known Dan. But Joshua Bearclaw was different from any man, any human being. He was a force she couldn't resist, an experience she couldn't avoid.

It was twilight now, and he was barely discernible. The motionless figure blended with rock and shadow, so that he almost disappeared. It would be like the rest of her life. Bearclaw would soon vanish, yet she would always know that he was there, just out of sight, just beyond reach.

Kira knew that her sad frame of mind wasn't fruitful. Bearclaw had his life, and she had hers. At the moment, Toby needed her. There was the ranch to sell and a career to build.

Turning from the window, she went to her son's room. He was sitting at his desk, his lamp burning brightly, bent over his schoolwork.

"Aren't you the busy beaver," she said.

Toby looked back. "Hi, Mom."

"Homework?" She looked over his shoulder. "Arithmetic, huh?"

He nodded. "Joshua said to do the hardest thing first. Always do the hardest thing."

"Your father is a wise man."

Toby looked up at her, leaning his chin on the back of the chair. "I'm not sorry I'm a Navaho, Mom."

"You shouldn't be. The Navahos are a good people."

"Joshua said if my heart is big and strong, nobody can hurt me. He said if I believe in something hard enough, I can have it, no matter what."

She stroked his head. "He's a strong man."

"Why won't he stay with us?"

"Because of what he believes in. His life is in Arizona, on the reservation."

Toby grimaced. "I guess what I believe in right now is arithmetic."

She laughed. "Well...can I take you away from your studies long enough for a hug?"

"Sure, Mom."

They sat side by side on the bed, their arms around each other. After a while, she realized they were clinging. Neither of them said anything, but they were sustaining each other. Despite what Joshua meant to them both, soon there would be only the two of them.

"Mom, would Joshua have come to the ranch if I wasn't his son?"

"Why no, honey. He wouldn't have had any reason to. Why do you ask?"

"He told me he liked you a lot, that I was lucky you're my mom."

A swell of happiness rose in her. "It's kind of Joshua to say that."

"Do you like him, too?"

"Yes, very much."

"Then why is he leaving?" He looked up at her.

How could she explain it, when she barely understood it herself? "I guess for the same reason he told you to do your arithmetic first. Sometimes you just have to do the hard thing."

Toby scratched his head. Before he could ask any more questions, they heard the sound of the front door. Moments later, Bearclaw appeared at the bedroom door. The light from the desk lamp cast dark shadows across his face. He smiled faintly at the sight of them, leaning his forearm against the door frame.

Kira realized she and Toby must have looked strange, perhaps a bit pathetic, holding on to each other. An unusual silence fell over the three of them.

"Did you have a good walk?" she finally asked.

"Yes. It was good to think." He studied them, his wolflike eyes gleaming in the shadows. His demeanor was resolute, but there was a gentleness to his voice.

"Do you want to talk?" she asked.

"I was wondering if I could borrow your Jeep."

Kira hesitated. She wanted to ask why, but putting him on the spot somehow seemed wrong. "Do you want to go into town?" she asked, risking the indirect approach.

"Yes. I won't be gone long."

There was no point in pushing him. "Will you have dinner before you leave?"

"I'd rather get going, if you don't mind."

She got up, patting Toby. She left the room, walking past Bearclaw to get her purse.

"How is your work coming, little brother?" she heard him ask. But she was beyond hearing for the reply.

Several moments later Joshua came into the front room. Kira handed him the keys to the Jeep. "Will you be all right?"

He smiled broadly, then touched her face with his palm. "Don't worry, I'll be fine."

Looking into his eyes, she felt her lip quiver. Then Bearclaw gathered her into his arms, holding her.

"I'm going to see if I can settle this thing," he said, knowing she wanted an explanation. "For Toby's sake and for yours."

She knew he wouldn't say more, so she didn't ask. He would tell her what he wanted her to know. He kissed her forehead, then went to the closet and took his jacket. She stood at the door with him.

"Can I come with you?"

He shook his head. "No, you stay with the boy." Giving her a final look, he walked into the night.

Kira waited up until eleven. When he didn't return, she decided to go to bed. She'd barely turned off the lights when she heard the Jeep in the driveway. Minutes later, she heard him in the hall, then in the bath.

She lay waiting for him to come to her. Finally the door opened, and he stepped into the room.

"Are you all right?" she whispered.

"Sorry, did I wake you?"

"I wasn't asleep. I was waiting up."

He sat on the side of the bed. Kira reached over and touched his face.

"Don't worry," he said, "no cuts or bruises."

She lay her head on his chest. "I was worried about you."

"There is no need. Everything's fine."

It was obvious he didn't want to discuss what he'd done. She kissed his neck, and he began stroking her head. His touch was light and soothing. It was as though she were a small animal. For a long time he caressed her. She felt he loved her.

"Kira," he whispered, "my little one."

When she went into the kitchen the next morning, Bearclaw was already rinsing his cup in the sink. He had on his suit, the one he'd worn to the hearing. His hair was shiny and combed back neatly.

"Why are you all dressed up?" she asked.

"I've got a meeting to attend."

"What meeting?"

"One I was invited to."

More secrecy, she realized. She took a mug from the cupboard and poured herself some coffee. "You want to borrow the Jeep again?"

"If you don't mind."

"Sure. Be my guest." She sat at the table.

"Don't be angry," he said, reading her mood. "It will all come out in good time."

Kira shrugged. "I know you've got your own business and aren't accountable to me. You don't owe me anything."

"I owe you a great deal."

She sipped her coffee, looking at him over the rim. "When will you be back?"

"If it goes all right, I'll stay in town until Toby is out of school. I'll bring him back with me."

"Okay, but I'll have to call Mr. Heartly and tell him you have my permission to pick him up."

"If you would, I'd be grateful. Please tell Toby to look for me outside the school." He glanced at his watch. "I have to hurry or I'll be late." He touched her hair, then turned and strode from the kitchen.

After he had gone, Kira got Toby up and off to the school bus. She couldn't imagine why Bearclaw had to be in town so early. She puttered around, worrying. Before lunch she walked down to the highway to check the mail. There was a utility bill, some junk mail and the books that she had ordered from the university library.

After eating a bowl of soup, she curled up in a chair and began reading the first book, feeling a sense of adventure. She knew that the study of Native American culture would become an important part of her life's work.

From her reading she quickly learned how interesting and rich the folkloric tradition of the Navaho was. It was an even more fascinating culture than she had realized. Wrapped up in her studies, she was surprised hours later to hear the Jeep. The time had gotten away from her. Toby and Bearclaw were home.

They came in the door, and by the expression on the boy's face, she saw that something had happened. He looked terribly sad.

"He's going, Mom," he announced somberly. "He's going back to Arizona."

Toby walked on back to his bedroom, leaving his father at the door. Kira looked at Bearclaw as she rose. She searched his eyes.

"They've dropped the charges," he explained. "One of the conditions is that I leave the state immediately."

She was dumbfounded. "Dropped the charges?"

He nodded, then stepped toward her. He seemed a bit stiff, distant. "I didn't explain everything to Toby," he said, lowering his voice, "but the gist of it is that Rod agreed to back down. The papers were signed this afternoon. I'm free to go."

The words hit her in the pit of the stomach. She had known that he would leave eventually, but she still wasn't prepared. All along she had been thinking about getting past the trial before having to face reality. "How did you get . . . ? Why did Rod agree to . . . ?"

He took her by the shoulders. "It's a long story, but the point is, he did. It's over now. You and Toby can get back to a normal life. That was my purpose."

"But Joshua—"

He shook his head. "It's better this way. I've been frustrated, handcuffed by the situation. But now I'm free. We all are."

"You have to leave? Now?"

"Yes. It will only be harder if I stay, even for a few hours. I'm going to pack. Then I'm leaving."

She was speechless. It took her a second to find something reasonable to ask. "Are you going to Medford?"

"Yes, I'll get on the first plane I can."

She felt her body tremble. "I'll drive you."

"I don't want you to. Besides, Toby needs you here. Taking him will just cause more upset. We've said goodbye. It's best if you both stay here."

"What are you going to do?"

"I'll hitch a ride. If I get down to the highway before it gets too late, I shouldn't have any trouble. I'm more presentable dressed like this than I was in jeans and boots."

"Joshua, it's ridiculous not to let me drive you. I can leave Toby with the Broyleses."

"No," he said, shaking his head. "I prefer it this way."

He went to the guest room to pack, and Kira stood alone in the front room. An empty feeling swept over her. She began pacing. After a few minutes Bearclaw returned, his bag in his hand.

"I insist on driving you to the highway. It's stupid to carry that bag a mile when you don't have to."

"All right. To the highway."

"You want to go now?" Her voice trembled with the words.

He nodded solemnly.

They went out to the vehicle. Kira got in and adjusted the seat. She looked at Bearclaw, who had climbed in beside her. "This is all very sudden," she said. "I guess I wasn't expecting it."

"It is better this way."

She started the engine and headed down the driveway toward the highway. It was a mile, but not nearly far enough. In a few minutes it would be over, he would be gone. Time never moved so inexorably, the end of something was never so dreaded, so near.

When she got to the highway, she pulled on the hand brake, left the engine running and got out of the Jeep. She walked around to where Bearclaw was just setting his case on the ground. She looked up at him. His gray eyes seemed to sink gently into her.

"Will you still be wanting to see Toby again?" she asked, her voice shaking.

"If you'll let me."

She managed a sad smile, nodding. "I guess you'll write to tell me what you have in mind."

"Yes."

"But don't surprise me like you did this trip, Joshua. Let's keep it businesslike next time. We probably shouldn't see each other. For both our sakes."

"As you wish."

She studied him, noting the faint pink line on his cheek, where he'd been cut in his fight with Rod. She knew it would fade until it was practically invisible one day, but for months he would look into the mirror and be reminded. Her sadness at the thought brought tears, despite the fact that she had steeled herself. "Everything was beautiful, Joshua," she murmured. "I'll always remember you."

His eyes were surprisingly intense. Then, without a word, he reached out and put his hand to her face. She watched him until her eyes began shimmering.

"The worst part is that I love you, Kira."

She took his fingers and held on to them with both hands. "It *is* the worst part, isn't it?" Her voice cracked on the last word, and tears ran down each cheek.

Bearclaw swallowed hard and his eyes welled. He leaned forward, kissing her ever so lightly. She took a deep breath, inhaling him for the last time. Then she turned and got back into the Jeep.

She didn't look at him again. She spun the vehicle around and headed back toward the ranch house. Nor did she glance into her rearview mirror. The tears were flowing heavily, and she wiped them away with the sleeve of her shirt.

When she got to the top of the bluff, she stopped and looked back. He was standing near the arched sign identifying the ranch, a speck in the distance. She faced forward again, but she couldn't just put the Jeep in the barn and return to the house. She had to know he'd gotten away.

Turning in a wide arc, she drove to a vantage point at the edge of the bluff, not far from where Joshua had burned the brush. There she sat, watching him in the afternoon sun. Kira knew she was torturing herself, but she couldn't help it.

Though the route was not heavily traveled, a number of vehicles passed. Finally, a truck stopped. Watching Joshua climb into the cab, the ache in her heart returned. She didn't know why she had tormented herself that way, watching him, but she needed to know he was off.

The truck moved slowly down the highway, toward Medford. She wondered if he was looking back at her and their mountain, or if in his mind and heart he was already on his way to Arizona and the life he'd planned. Did it hurt him as much as it hurt her? Did he really love her?

Fourteen

———

A week after Bearclaw left, Mr. Sorenson, the man who'd contracted to buy the ranch, came with Al Kinney and some other men to thoroughly inspect the property. Al had called from town to warn her not to get excited when a helicopter landed in her front yard. Still, Kira couldn't help but be amazed at the sight of the aircraft hovering outside her parents' home, kicking up dust in all directions.

As she watched, four men emerged from the chopper. Two headed off toward the barn, another man and Al Kinney came up to the house. Kira met them on the porch. The broker introduced Mr. Sorenson, a thin little man in his sixties, who wore wire-rimmed glasses, jeans and boots and carried a cowboy hat in his hand.

"We won't be disturbing you for long, Mrs. Lowell," he said amiably. "We've inspected the rangeland and pastures by air. I just want a quick look at the buildings and improvements."

Kira shrugged. "Whatever you wish. Would you care to see the house?"

"If you don't mind."

She gestured toward the open door. "Be my guest."

Al stayed with her on the porch, grinning as he looked out at the helicopter. "The man certainly does things right."

"Let's hope it means he's serious about buying the place," she said.

"Can't say for sure yet, but I have a good feeling about the deal."

Kira rubbed her arms against the cool air. Autumn, it seemed, had arrived in a hurry. "Let's hope so."

"I understand that friend of yours, the Indian fella, is gone," the broker said in an offhand way. "What was his name?"

"Bearclaw. Joshua Bearclaw."

"That's right." Kinney rose up on his toes, his hands thrust in his pockets as he looked out at the chopper. "I don't know what kind of a lawyer he is, but he's got guts, I've got to hand that much to him."

She looked at him with surprise. "What do you mean?"

"That speech he gave at the Chamber of Commerce meeting, when he ate humble pie in front of pretty near the whole town."

"What are you talking about?"

"Didn't you know? At our meeting last week, Conrad Willoughby introduced this Bearclaw fella, who got up and publicly apologized to Rod Banyon."

"Apologized? At a meeting?"

"Yeah. Said he was sorry about assaulting Rod and the grief he brought him. I figured you must have known."

A surge of anger went through her. "No, I didn't. I had no idea."

About then Mr. Sorenson came out of the house. He said some polite things, but Kira barely heard him, she was so angry. She pulled herself together enough to shake hands before the men headed toward the barn. Then she went into the house. After pacing back and forth for a while, she picked up the phone and called Rod at his office.

"Well, well, I was wondering if I'd ever hear from you again," he said smugly.

"What happened with Joshua at the Chamber of Commerce meeting last week?"

"You mean he didn't tell you? I thought the two of you were such good friends that you'd share everything."

"I'm not interested in your sarcasm. What happened?"

He laughed. "I was surprised he had the nerve to come to the meeting. I guess he didn't have enough to tell you, though."

"Quit being evasive!"

"All right. The bastard asked what it would take to get me to drop the charges. I told him I'd be glad to see his butt in the slammer, and he says we both knew he wasn't going to jail. He said if humiliating him was what I wanted, why wasn't there something else that would please me just as much."

"So you made him stand up in front of the town and apologize."

"He didn't have to. I told him if fighting was what I was interested in, I'd have whipped him at the motel. I brought the charges to preserve my dignity. That's the truth, Kira."

"I don't give a damn about your dignity. What did Joshua say at the meeting?" She could hear Rod's breathing over the line. He was growing angry.

"He told everybody the truth. Said he'd assaulted me, that it was his fault, and that if I hadn't held back, it'd have been much worse. Then he apologized to the community for the trouble he caused."

"Rod, you're a lowlife, you really are," she said, seething. "That fight was your doing. You took advantage of him to humiliate him publicly. It was blackmail."

"Listen, Kira, he came to me. If he was in the right, he could have proved it in court. He's damned lucky I was willing to drop the charges, and he knew it."

She felt hot tears of anger. "He crawled to you to spare his son pain and humiliation. And he wanted to spare me, too. He wanted to spare me the trouble of calling you a liar in court!"

"Well, aren't we the holy one. What did you give him for your promise? That's what I'd like to know."

She was so enraged she couldn't answer. Rod was so vile, she couldn't even tell him how despicable he was. Without a word, she slammed down the phone. Then she went back into the front room, wringing her hands with frustration.

Poor Joshua. He was so proud. How hard it must have been for him to grovel in front of the likes of Rod Banyon. She knew why he had done it. For them. When Toby had been taunted by the other children, Bearclaw decided to end the thing as quickly as possible. He sacrificed to do it.

Kira had an overwhelming urge to call him, to tell him how sorry she was, and how grateful. He deserved that much. She wanted him to know that what he'd done had solved the problem. Toby had been somber all week, but there hadn't been anymore trouble at school. It would take a while for the wounds to heal, but Joshua had been right.

His leaving had changed the atmosphere immediately, and things would be back to normal soon.

But how could she contact him? He hadn't left an address or a phone number. It hadn't even occurred to her to ask. His leaving had seemed so definitive. It had even been left up to him if he would see Toby again.

Certain she could track him down through the tribal authorities, Kira called the Navaho reservation in Arizona. A clerk in the offices on the tribal counsel advised her to write, indicating she had no telephone listing for Joshua Bearclaw.

And so she wrote, telling him that she respected him for what he had done, and that she was terribly sorry about the ordeal he had gone through. She told him that Toby was doing well. The trouble in school had apparently passed. Whatever scars Toby might carry were more than made up for by what he had gained in knowing his father. She closed saying that she loved him.

Once the letter was off, Kira waited, not knowing what to expect. His sacrifice, her words of thanks and her expression of love weighed on her, keeping him constantly in her thoughts. She had hoped that Joshua Bearclaw would slowly fade from her mind, but he didn't. The fact that there was no early reply to her letter made her wonder. She didn't want to forget him. She hoped, because of Toby, he might somehow continue to play a role in her life.

She worried, too, that she might have misread the situation. Had she taken their relationship more seriously than he? Though she didn't doubt his sincerity, Kira reluctantly came to the conclusion that Joshua had simply managed to put things into perspective, whereas she hadn't—not the way she needed to.

She made an effort to look to the future. She read and studied incessantly. It was as though informing herself about Indian culture was the best way to deal with her loss.

One sunny afternoon she took several hours off and climbed the mountain where she had gone with him that day. She sat by the waterfall, bundled in a warm jacket, listening to the water and watching the boughs of the trees swaying overhead. It felt right to honor what they'd shared.

Al Kinney called after a few weeks to inform her that the sale of the ranch was firm. The closing date was set for January 3. The news left her with a sense of relief. Kira felt it was time to move on. She had flirted with the idea of settling down in her hometown but, deep down, she had known it would never work.

Kira wrote to the university in San Diego for an application to the masters program in anthropology, and she redoubled her reading regimen. A few days after Thanksgiving, a letter came from Bearclaw. There was a short note to Toby, which she gave to the boy, and a somewhat longer one to her, together with a money order for fifty dollars.

Dear Kira,
Your words about my son warmed my heart. I have thought of you both so many times over the past weeks. My life is not the same as it was before I went to Oregon, nor am I the same man.

I am sending some money to help with the expenses from my stay at your home. I will send more in the future, which you might want to put in a fund for Toby's education. I see it as my responsibility to him and to you.

I have wondered often about the sale of your ranch and what your plans might be for the future. Please let me know what happens with you, especially if you plan to leave Oregon. I want always to know where you are.

It was very hard to leave you, Kira. Since then my sleep has not come easily. I have learned also that the work I have chosen will be difficult, as I planned it. There are many things in my mind now, many questions about my life.

You said in your letter that you love me, and the words made my heart soar when I read them. But it saddened me, also, because it would be easier for me to know that I passed from your life as the winter snows in the warm days of spring.

What can we do with this love but cherish it? It can never change the people we are or the world we live in. I have pondered this so often but never find the answer, yet my love for you will not die. It cannot.

Please know that my greatest joy is knowing that my son is in your hands and that he has your love.

                                        Joshua Bearclaw

Kira fought back her tears, reading the letter over and over. She let it sit on her dresser for several days before she answered it. She informed Bearclaw about the sale of the ranch and her intention to move to San Diego after the Christmas holidays. She also told him about her plans to return to the university to study Native American culture.

She ended by expressing how moved she was by his words, though she knew that an impossible love was the worst kind. It was better for them not to torture each other with things that could not be.

The words were not easy for her to write, but it was a sentiment she thought he needed—and perhaps wanted—to hear. Expressing her love, as she had in her first letter, was honest, but it wasn't kind. She resolved to do what was right.

They did not hear from Bearclaw again until just before the holidays, when a parcel arrived. There was a small Christmas gift for Toby, another check for fifty dollars and a note indicating a new address and a telephone number in Flagstaff. Kira was curious about the address change, because it meant he wasn't living on the reservation. Bearclaw did ask that she send him her new address in San Diego, though there was nothing more. He had taken her cue, perhaps gratefully. It seemed their relationship was finally getting into perspective.

The day after Christmas, Kira left Toby with the Broyleses and flew to San Diego to find a place for them to live. She had decided to buy another house eventually, but she thought it would be best to rent for a while first until she was sure of the area she wanted to be in. The second day she found an apartment in La Jolla, two blocks from a nice elementary school and just a couple of miles from the university.

Returning to Oregon, Kira began packing in earnest. She had done quite a bit through the weeks, but the job had to be finished in time for the movers, who were due at the end of the week. The moving company came to pick up the boxes and the few pieces of furniture belonging to her parents that she wished to keep. The rest was sold or given to charity. She got rid of the Jeep, deciding it wasn't as practical for Southern California as it had been for Oregon. On New Year's Eve morning, Ed and Louise Broyles drove Kira and Toby to Medford for their flight to San Diego.

They stayed in a motel in La Jolla for a couple of days. Kira bought a car, and the day before their things were due to arrive from Oregon, she dropped Toby off with some old friends, then went by the apartment to make sure it was clean and ready to be occupied.

A few pieces of mail had already been forwarded from Seneca Falls. One letter bore the return address of the Navaho tribal council. With trembling hands, she tore the envelope open. It was what she had been fearing for months. The tribe was asserting its jurisdiction over Toby.

Kira sank to the floor in the empty living room of her apartment, her back against the wall, the letter in her hands. She read it again more carefully, scrutinizing each word for indications of the seriousness of the development. From what Conrad Willoughby said, she knew it didn't necessarily mean they would take Toby away from her, but she was still scared. The fact that they wanted their say was enough to frighten her. What did it mean, and why were they doing it now, after all these years?

She thought immediately of Bearclaw. He might be able to help her. But then she stopped herself. Could he somehow be behind this?

A panicky feeling went through her. Joshua couldn't do anything like that, knowing how it would hurt her. Or could he? They both knew they had no future together. His commitment to his people, his chosen way of life, left no room for her. They had known that from the beginning. He had said he wanted Toby to be with her, but perhaps he'd changed his mind. Maybe the harsh reality of their disparate lives had changed his thinking.

Kira got up and went to the sliding glass door, hating what she was thinking. She hated herself for doubting. Yet the letter was in her hand. Someone had brought Toby to the attention of the tribal authorities.

Outside, the sky was darkening with heavy gray clouds. A winter storm had been predicted, and Kira could see it was on the way. The wind was kicking up the palm fronds, and the shrubs bent and swayed in the rising gale. Soon she'd have to pick up her son. But before then she'd contact the lawyer who'd handled the adoption. If she was going to have a fight on her hands, she knew she'd have to be prepared.

She decided not to tell Toby about the letter from the tribe until after they'd settled in. The lawyer's secretary told Kira he would be in court and unavailable for consultation until the end of the week. They scheduled an appointment, and Kira devoted herself to settling into their new home.

The movers arrived with their things and the furniture that she'd had in storage. The telephone was connected, the meters for the utilities were read. There was a semblance of order.

Since the kitchen things weren't unpacked, she and Toby went out for pizza, then returned to their apartment. The boy was tired and went to bed early. Kira sat in the living room amid the boxes, feeling frightened and a little disoriented. She kept thinking about the letter, getting it out of her purse to read again. Without more facts she couldn't hold Bearclaw responsible. Still, she couldn't help feeling betrayed. Even if only in some small way, he had to be responsible.

The storm finally blew in from the Pacific, and the rain began pelting the sliding door leading to their tiny balcony. Kira closed the drapes and curled up in a chair, feeling vulnerable and alone. She reminded herself of Conrad Willoughby's words that she would be in a strong position to keep Toby, even if it came to a court action.

But she wondered if in the cases where a child had been with the adoptive parents for a long time, there was a natural parent who loved the child as much as Bearclaw loved Toby.

There was no point in torturing herself, yet she couldn't help being scared. It crossed her mind to try to reach Bearclaw, to confront him, but she saw nothing to be gained. It there was to be a confrontation, it would come soon enough. Besides, he could always come to her.

She remembered then that he'd asked her to give him their new address. Obviously, he'd wanted to keep track of Toby, but deep in her heart she'd been hoping it was because he wanted to keep in touch with her, as well. All that seemed academic now. It didn't help to remind herself she had no proof he was responsible. She was afraid to trust his love.

Fifteen

It rained all the next day, the water drumming incessantly against the windowpane. Kira walked Toby to school with the umbrella, and she planned to pick him up that afternoon. He could have gone by himself, but since the letter had arrived, she was feeling very possessive. She still hadn't told him of their problem, but knew she had to soon. She resolved not to put it off any longer. She would tell him that night.

Back at the apartment, Kira rolled up her sleeves and went to work, knowing it was important to keep busy. She was putting dishes in the cupboard when the phone rang. It was Louise Broyles.

"Honey, I just had to call you. I don't know if I did the right thing, but I didn't sleep last night, worrying."

"About what? What's happened?"

"Toby's father called last night. Ed was at a meeting of his sports club, or I'd have had him talk. I did the best I could, but I don't know if I did right."

"Louise, what did you do?"

"I gave him your address in San Diego."

There was a silence on the line, and Kira felt the weight of the moment. "I take it he asked for it...."

"Yes, he said he was trying urgently to get ahold of you and that the phone over at your parents' place was disconnected. I explained that you'd moved. He said he knew that, but that you hadn't yet sent him the new address. He made it sound very important, so I gave it to him." She paused. "Was that all right to do, Kira?"

She was thinking, and it took her a second to respond. "Yes, Louise. I was planning on writing to him." She could see no reason to upset her. Of more immediate concern was Joshua. Why was he trying to contact her?

"At first I thought that was the case, but then I got to thinking maybe you wouldn't want him to know. I never said anything to you about all the talk in town when he was here—it was none of my business—but then I knew he left under...difficult circumstances, so I started worrying. Ed said it wouldn't matter, but I just had to let you know in case it was a problem."

"Thanks, Louise, I'm glad you did. But there's nothing to worry about."

Louise seemed relieved when the conversation ended, which is the way Kira wanted her to feel, though she *was* alarmed. She had no reason to believe Bearclaw meant any harm, but the situation was so confused, and she felt so insecure, she didn't know what to think.

At noon she finished arranging the bathroom and was just going to the kitchen to heat up some soup for lunch, when there was a knock at the door. She hesitated, then realized it was probably the building manager, who had promised her a second set of keys to the apartment. When she opened the door, she found Joshua Bearclaw standing in the hall.

She froze, fear touching her. But she realized that his expression, though sober, didn't justify her alarm. Looking into his eyes, she saw the man she had loved, not one who was threatening to take her child.

"Hello, Joshua," she said when he didn't speak.

"I'm sorry to come like this," he said, "but I had to see you."

"Louise told me you had talked to her." They stared silently at each other. "It's about Toby and the court. That's why you've come, isn't it?"

He nodded.

Kira's eyes slid down him. He wore a trench coat, and under it a suit and tie. His face and hair were wet from the rain. His eyes shone intently from the comparative darkness of the hallway.

"You want him, don't you?" she said.

"No. That's why I came. I want to tell you this is not my doing. I wanted to warn you. But when I found out about it, I was already too late."

"You didn't initiate it?"

He shook his head.

Kira wanted to believe him, but she was afraid to hope, to trust her desires. The emotion of the situation suddenly caught up with her. "I prayed you weren't behind it," she said with a shaky voice, "but I knew how much you loved Toby."

"Please, Kira, you've got to believe me. If I could have prevented this, I would. The last thing I want is to put you both through this. The very last thing."

"Really?" Tears had formed. Her voice was weak, thin.

For the first time since she'd opened the door, he moved, stepping forward to take her into his arms. The front of his coat was wet, but she didn't care. At that moment she needed his comfort and his love more than anything on earth. Feeling his strength, she let go and began to cry.

"Ever since the letter came," she sobbed, "I've been terrified. I was afraid that you were involved, that you decided to take him away from me."

"No, never. I'd give up seeing him myself before I would let that happen to you." He kissed her tear-streaked cheek and closed the door.

"You're wet." He removed his trench coat, and she took it to the kitchen, then returned.

He looked so handsome and dignified, almost a different man than the one she'd known in Oregon. And yet, under the sophisticated veneer was the same man who had mesmerized her with his quiet strength. Watching him, she recalled his tender affection, the strange mixture of raw animal force and gentle love he'd shown her when they'd been intimate.

Joshua must have been remembering, too, because he was staring at her. After a moment, he lifted her chin with his finger and kissed her lips. "I've missed you," he whispered.

She savored the taste and feel of him. She held back for a moment or two then threw herself against him, kissing him as eagerly as he began kissing her. And when the caress was over, she lay her head on his shoulder and held him, her arms around his waist. He stroked her head.

"The past few days have been miserable," she said, her voice cracking. "I hated the thought we might be enemies again."

"We've never been enemies. It's always been fear and uncertainty. That's all."

"What about the tribal court? How do I know I'll win?"

"They haven't said they want to take him from you. They're just trying to track down all the children who've left the tribe, so they can make a determination. It's only a step," he said. "And we'll deal with it together."

She pulled back. "Is that why you came, Joshua?"

He looked at her for a long moment, then he released her and walked to the sliding glass door, watching the rain. Kira stared at his back, knowing that what he was thinking was terribly important.

"I wrote to you that I wasn't living on the reservation. Now I'm ready to explain why." He hadn't turned around. He was staring out at the gray rain-drenched sky.

She waited.

"When I returned to Arizona, I discovered I wasn't the Navaho I thought I was. Like many of my people, I have been a stranger in the white man's world. With a college education and law school, I became a knowledgeable stranger. But when I fell in love with you, I wanted to become a part of your world, even though I knew I didn't belong in it." He turned to face her.

She saw that his eyes were glistening. "Oh, Joshua..."

"These past months I've been trying to figure out who I am, what I want. I knew I could never live a life going to meetings and doing business with people like Rod Banyon—"

"Rod is not the best representative of our world, Joshua. He's despicable. There are many good people in every culture, in every society."

"I realize that. That is not what I meant. What I am trying to say is, I couldn't abandon my people for the Chamber of Commerce, nor, I've discovered, could I live among them—at least not without you. I know you can't become an Indian any more than I can become a white man. So for the past month I have been working on a compromise."

"What sort of compromise?"

"Before I told you my plan, I wanted to find out if I could make it work. Unfortunately, this tribal action involving Toby came up before I finished what I wanted to do."

"You can tell me about it. Even if you're not sure."

"I'm sure of my feelings. That's not the issue. I wanted to be a little further along in my plans, that's all. I know more than ever how important you are to me."

"Joshua, what is it? What have you done?"

"I have taken a position in a law firm in Flagstaff. It's a prominent firm, a civic-minded firm. Because of the large Native American population and high unemployment among my people, there is much to be done. The firm recognizes it has a responsibility to contribute to the effort. I'll run that side of the practice. I'll do other things, as well, but mainly I'll work in the interest of the Navaho, the Hopi and other tribes."

"That's wonderful!"

"I have one foot on the reservation, one foot in Flagstaff. It's all very new. We're just starting, but I believe I can make it work."

"I hope you find a way to live that makes you happy."

He walked over to her, taking her face in his hands. "I made another discovery these past months, as well. I cannot live for my work alone. The happiest days of my life have been those when we were together. It I can't be happy on the reservation, and if I can't be happy in Flagstaff, it's because I do not have you."

She felt a lump of emotion in her throat, and her eyes filled. Bearclaw leaned over and tenderly kissed her lips.

"I love you, little one," he whispered.

She threw her arms around him and held him tightly. "And I love you." The words came out as a sob.

They stood for a long time holding each other, listening to the rain.

"Let me show you something," he said, taking a booklet from his inside coat pocket. He handed it to her. "This is the course catalogue for Northern Arizona University in Flagstaff." A crinkly smile touched his lips. "There are many classes offered on the Native Americans. And because of the location of the town, there are jobs for people who are knowledgeable of both cultures."

"What are you trying to say, Joshua?"

"I think you should come to Arizona."

"So that if I lose in court I can visit Toby at your house?"

He smiled. "Or so that if you win, I can visit him at yours."

"You don't like coming all the way to San Diego, I take it."

He touched her nose. "There's another possibility. You can marry me, then we won't have to worry about any of that. My place is modest, but it's not a hogan. It has three bedrooms and two bathrooms. There's a fireplace in the living room and a sprinkler system out in the yard. An accountant lives on one side of me and a paving contractor on the other."

"Can you really live that way, Joshua?"

"I can't live any other way." He grinned. "Besides, the building contractor is half Hopi and he has three kids who are a quarter Hopi. He's promised a friendly rivalry."

"In the number of kids?"

"No, he's got too big a head start. Anyway, he knows I'm single. But I told him I was going to San Diego to find a wife."

She looked into his magical eyes. "Is that a proposal, or a lawyerly negotiation?"

He smiled. "Since I no longer fight, I have learned to be shrewd."

Kira put her arms around his neck. "It's okay not to fight," she whispered. "But I hope you haven't given up making love."

He nuzzled her playfully. "When does our son get home from school?"

She pressed her moist lips against his neck. "Not for a long, long time."

*   *   *   *   *

"GIVE YOUR HEART TO SILHOUETTE" SWEEPSTAKES
OFFICIAL RULES
NO PURCHASE NECESSARY TO ENTER OR RECEIVE A PRIZE

1. To enter and join the Silhouette Reader Service, rub off the concealment device on all game tickets. This will reveal the potential value for each Sweepstakes entry number and the number of free book(s) you will receive. Accepting the free book(s) will automatically entitle you to also receive a free bonus gift. If you do not wish to take advantage of our introduction to the Silhouette Reader Service but wish to enter the Sweepstakes only, rub off the concealment device on tickets #1-3 only. To enter, return your entire sheet of tickets. Incomplete and/or inaccurate entries are not eligible for that section or section (s) of prizes. Not responsible for mutilated or unreadable entries or inadvertent printing errors. Mechanically reproduced entries are null and void.

2. Either way, your Sweepstakes numbers will be compared against the list of winning numbers generated at random by computer. In the event that all prizes are not claimed, random drawings will be made from all entries received from all presentations to award all unclaimed prizes. All cash prizes are payable in U.S. funds. This is in addition to any free, surprise or mystery gifts that might be offered. The following prizes are awarded in this sweepstakes:

(1)	*Grand Prize	$1,000,000 Annuity
(1)	First Prize	$35,000
(1)	Second Prize	$10,000
(3)	Third Prize	$5,000
(10)	Fourth Prize	$1,000
(25)	Fifth Prize	$500
(5000)	Sixth Prize	$5

   *The Grand Prize is payable through a $1,000,000 annuity. Winner may elect to receive $25,000 a year for 40 years, totaling up to $1,000,000 without interest, or $350,000 in one cash payment. Winners selected will receive the prizes offered in the Sweepstakes promotion they receive.
   Entrants may cancel the Reader Service privileges at any time without cost or obligation to buy (see details in center insert card).

3. Versions of this Sweepstakes with different graphics may be offered in other mailings or at retail outlets by Torstar Corp. and its affiliates. This promotion is being conducted under the supervision of Marden-Kane, Inc., an independent judging organization. By entering this Sweepstakes, each entrant accepts and agrees to be bound by these rules and the decisions of the judges, which shall be final and binding. Odds of winning are dependent upon the total number of entries received. Taxes, if any, are the sole responsibility of the winners. Prizes are nontransferable. All entries must be received by March 31, 1990. The drawing will take place on April 30, 1990, at the offices of Marden-Kane, Inc., Lake Success, N.Y.

4. This offer is open to residents of the U.S., Great Britain and Canada, 18 years or older, except employees of Torstar Corp., its affiliates, and subsidiaries, Marden-Kane, Inc. and all other agencies and persons connected with conducting this Sweepstakes. All federal, state and local laws apply. Void wherever prohibited or restricted by law.

5. Winners will be notified by mail and may be required to execute an affidavit of eligibility and release that must be returned within 14 days after notification. Canadian winners will be required to answer a skill-testing question. Winners consent to the use of their name, photograph and/or likeness for advertising and publicity in conjunction with this and similar promotions without additional compensation. One prize per family or household.

6. For a list of our most current major prizewinners, send a stamped, self-addressed envelope to: WINNERS LIST, c/o MARDEN-KANE, INC., P.O. BOX 701, SAYREVILLE, N.J. 08871

If Sweepstakes entry form is missing, please print your name and address on a 3" ×5" piece of plain paper and send to

In the U.S.

Sweepstakes Entry
901 Fuhrmann Blvd
P.O. Box 1867
Buffalo, NY 14269-1867

In Canada

Sweepstakes Entry
P.O. Box 609
Fort Erie, Ontario
L2A 5X3

LTY-S69R

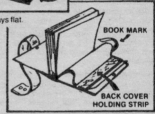

 **Silhouette Desire** ®

COMING NEXT MONTH

#505 ODD MAN OUT—Lass Small
July's *Man of the Month*, Graham Rawlins, was undeniably attractive, but Roberta Lambert seemed uninterested. However, Graham was very determined, and she found he'd do almost *anything* to get her attention....

#506 THE PIRATE O'KEEFE—Helen R. Myers
Doctor Laura Connell was intrigued by the injured man washed up on her beach. When she discovered his true identity it was too late—she'd fallen for the pirate O'Keefe.

#507 A WILDER NAME—Laura Leone
Luke Swain was positively the most irritating man Nina Gnagnarelli had ever met. He'd insulted her wardrobe, her integrity and her manners. He'd also set her heart on fire!

#508 BLIND JUSTICE—Cathryn Clare
As far as Lily Martineau was concerned, successful corporate lawyer Matt Malone was already married—to his job. Matt pleaded guilty as charged, then demanded a retrial.

#509 ETERNALLY EVE—Ashley Summers
Nate Wright had left Eve Sheridan with a broken heart. Now he seemed to have no memory of her—but it was a night Eve would never forget!

#510 MAGIC TOUCH—Noelle Berry McCue
One magic night with a handsome stranger made Caroline Barclay feel irresistible. But she didn't believe in fairy tales until James Mitchel walked back into her life—as her new boss.

AVAILABLE NOW:

Coming in July from

Silhouette Desire®

ODD MAN OUT #505
by Lass Small

Roberta Lambert is too busy with her job to notice that her new apartment-mate is a strong, desirable man. But Graham Rawlins has ways of getting her undivided attention....

Roberta is one of five fascinating Lambert sisters. She is as enticing as each one of her three sisters, whose stories you have already enjoyed or will want to read:

- Hillary in GOLDILOCKS AND THE BEHR (Desire #437)
- Tate in HIDE AND SEEK (Desire #453)
- Georgina in RED ROVER (Desire #491)

Watch for Book IV of Lass Small's terrific miniseries and read Fredricka's story in TAGGED (Desire #528) coming in October.